T0130509

# A Tribute to Bullying:

## "What They Call Ugly"

✳ ✳ ✳

# Susan Horton

authorHOUSE®

AuthorHouse™
1663 Liberty Drive
Bloomington, IN 47403
www.authorhouse.com
Phone: 1-800-839-8640

Published by AuthorHouse 2/7/2012

ISBN: 978-1-4678-4881-7 (e)
ISBN: 978-1-4678-4882-4 (sc)

To Pain,
my ultimate inspiration...
in some form or another.

# Foreword

I know what it's like to be imprisoned by fear.

I know what it's like to be strangled by loneliness and inadequacy.

I know the pain of not being normal.

I know how long a night can seem when there is just a promise of day.

I am writing this book for those who have no voice to cry out.

This is not a tell-all book about events that may or may not have happened. In fact, all of these characters are fictional. The words came to me while I was driving my bus, or cutting an onion to go in my oxtails. Just about all of these stories are dreams that awoke me physically and spiritually. The revelation in these stories is not only a vice to call attention to the ugliness of society, but it is also serving as warning to those who inflict the pain of ridicule. Do not assume that this excludes you.

For how many of us have taunted someone for being different? I have learned that hurtful words or harsh judgments do not come from sound minds, and the aggressors are often victims of their own low self-esteem. Most of the people who are the tormentors of *what they call ugly*, are they themselves the epitome of what they criticize.

Webster defines "ugly" in two ways; as an adjective and as an adverb. Basic English tells us that an adjective describes a noun, and an adverb describes a verb or an action. This book is using the context of both. The first definition of ugly is offensive to the sight or unpleasant to any sense. That is the obvious understanding. The second and most over looked is morally offensive or objectionable behavior; surly; likely to cause an inconvenience or discomfort; i.e. the ugly truth.

My brothers and sisters, this includes everyone. This not only describes in a somewhat grotesque detail the victimization of those who display characteristics that cause the offense to our sight, but also talks about the bullies whose morally objectionable behavior causes discomfort and inconvenience to their prey.

The root of the word is from the Old Norse *ugga*, which means to fear. As I read this, it made perfect sense to me. We are afraid! Isn't that the emotion that we are really displaying when we mistreat someone who is different? We can't fix them, we can't change what they look like, smell like, think like, act like, walk like, etc. so we do what our instincts are innately built to do: fight or flight. We become aggressive, and malicious towards that difference, because there, but for the grace of an almighty GOD, go us. And to seal the venomous attack we take flight emotionally. We distance ourselves from their humanity so that the inhumane treatment seems logical. Some good looking guy will see a large woman and will think to himself; she's fat, so she can't feel it when I take advantage of her finances, and ravage her emotionally. He will say she's not normal so she is expendable. That is just like bouncing a ball on a wall. What if those bricks were to yell out, "Hey man quit hitting me with that damn ball!" Sadly, some of you would be more inclined to have mercy on that wall, than on a wall of woman. He got a club foot, an esthetically pleasing female would probably think, "Shit, he should be happy I'm even talking to his limping ass." These are examples of how an adjective provokes an adverb. So who's right? The answer is neither and both. We are guilty and innocent at the same time. I am not trying to right a wrong, but simply advising so you can govern yourselves accordingly.

ENJOY!

# Table of Contents

\*\*\*

# Ugly is in the eye of the eye of the beholder

\*\*\*

# A Tree's Life

"Alright angel, but this is the last time. You don't want Granny to come in here with that switch do you?" Poppy asked with a smile on his gentle face.

I tilted my head and chirped matter of factly, "Granny wouldn't spank me for listening to a story!"

"She wouldn't whoop you, she would get me! She would claim I'm keeping you up past your bedtime again. One more time missy then it's off to dreamland with you!" He scooped me up in his arms and sat down in that old rocking chair. This was our time...mine and Poppy's. He would hold me in his arms and tell me tales of how it used to be. Most of the stories he told me I sealed away in my memory. I wanted to remember him forever. He would always remind me that our time together wasn't long, and that he needed someone to keep his memories alive when that time came to an end.

*There once was an old sharecropping woman named Alice Mae. She lived in a town called Sweetwater Bay. Alice Mae was a very unusual woman. They say she was the descendant of slaves who bought they own freedom by breeding and selling their own children. Once they became masters, they bought back all they ones they could find and freed them. It was rumored that her family founded Sweetwater Bay and hired a white man to run their township. As is the nature of these greedy tyrants, they stole the land right out from under these blacks and leased it back to them. Knowing what a contribution her folks made to this town, Alice Mae scrimped and saved every nickel she could lay hold of, and bought back her families' land; plot by plot. Once she did this she had very little money left to hire hands to whip it back into shape. So she married the first man to come along an began breeding. This was not an unsual practice. Folks rarely married for love. If you were the right height, weight and complexion, shoot you was a shoe in for a mate. Back then folks married and had children to work the land and turn a profit. Since her future family of helpin' hands was afar off, she and her new husband took to the fields and started clearing trees and brush to get the fields ready for plowing. Now Alice Mae was in her 5th month of trevail and the heat started* getting to her, so she took shade under an old oak tree. This tree was solid as they come, and its trunk bore the scars of that times woes. She had packed a knap sack with a salmon biscuit and a baked sweet potato. She also kept a jug of fresh water to wet her throat in that swelterin' heat. 'Midst all the consumables she also carried an ax. Even though she was with child, Alice Mae was a sturdy woman who was able to chop down a tree as good as any man. As she sat under that old oak, she heard a cry. Sounded like a wounded animal at first, then it sounded like a woman weeping. Not sure what to expect, Alice Mae grabbed that ax and called, "Who dat?" After lookin' round for a few minutes, she settled in to have a bite to eat. Once again she heard sobbing, and like clockwork she bounded to her feet and grabbed that old ax. "sho yo'sef, fo I put dis' herr ax to good use!" Just like before, there was no one around. Alice Mae chunked that last bite of salmon biscuit in her mouth, took a long swig from that jug of water an commenced to workin' on the land. She cleared some small brush and debris from the area and decided to save that old tree for last. Well sir, as the day went on she got plenty of work done. The time came to chop down that old tree. Alice Mae liked to pretend that a tree was the crooks who stole her heritage out from under her. That's how she was able to bring 'em down so fast and with so much strength. She walked around it once to size it up, then she gave it her *ususal speech, 'looka herr Mr. Tree, t'ain't nothin' personal, jus' tryna take back wat wuz took from me." This time the tree answered back:*

"James Parker!" Granny interrupted. "'That child gotta go to school tomorrow! It's bedtime!" I know that she didn't mean any harm but her timing was terrible.

"Please Granny!" I begged. "I just gotta hear what happens next."

"No! It's bedtime and you have got to get up early in the morning." She said as she busied herself laying out my uniform.

"Awww Emma I'll be done in a minute. I was almost at the end anyhow. Let us have a few more minutes. You know she the only one who listens to these old stories of mine." Poppy hung his head as he uttered these last words.

I place my hands on his shoulder and said, "It's ok Poppy. I'll remember them,... even after you're dead!" He then looked at me and grabbed me in a very dramatic embrace. We both began to hold each other and make weeping noises.

"Alright you two hams! Just a few more minutes and then it's off to sleep with you young lady!" she chimed as she turned to leave the room.

We both fall back into our place. "Ok. Where was I? Oh yeah..."

*"Ms. Alice, I been out here for as long as you can remember. I was a sapling when your folks*

*bought this land. I remember the coo when it was taken out from under them. I was still green at the time, but I helped them take what was rightfully yours. See I was planted on this soil to benefit the cause of the white man. Before I could even break through the dirt, he enlisted me in his army against integration and the advancement of colored people. I don't have any feeling one way or another about white or black, but I was a soldier. I followed orders and held my position. (Just then that old willow started to mist) GOD put instructions in my seed and gave me to obey man. So I did just that. Like the time they hung Edgar and Laney's boy from my branches. I thought that was a bit extreme, but I had been enlisted in the struggle, so I held that noose up as high as I could so it would be over quick and afterward I held him up so they could find him and bring down right proper. Then there was the time they burned Leroy alive. I cradled him right here in this nook while the flames ate away at his flesh. I even provided shade to them while they tarred a little colored girl for stealing bread. I have seen quite a few whipped to death with all the fear and torment that could be mustered up by any man. There was Georgie, Lem, Whistler, Timmy, Lil' Earl, Fish, Tobias, Jim, Ol' Tom, Billy, Roosevelt, Eddra, Timothy, Jaboe, Larry, Tater Mae, Bo Jessie, Marvina, Jeffries, Black Ben, Drucilla, Cephus, Rhema, Pie, Leon, Uncle Jim, Tobias, Nellie, Paul, Dancing Joe, Mont, Miss Rose, Ann T, Cat, Aunt*

*Gussie, Big Eli, Vera, Ken, Fat Mike, Mo, Frank Jr., Alberta, Bay Mae, Josiah, Hawk, One Leg Sam, Willie Mae, Tom Cat, Sadie, Lily, Lewis, Charlie Mac, Tren , Coot, Micheal James, Bertha, Mae Mae, Franklin, ReeRee, Sumna, Mitchell, Levy, Terry, and some more. Each of these died in my arms and I embraced each one as best I could. Now I know it's time for me to serve in a different way. I gladly lay down my life for a different cause. I stood for segregation and hatred, now I will die for retribution and restoration." Alice Mae looked at that old tree, put her hand on its trunk and said, "I forgive you." Then with all the force and strength GOD would give a five month pregnant woman, she swung that ax and lay blade to that tree until it hit the ground. She took wood from that old willow and framed the door way to their first home on their newly reclaimed land. That winter she gave birth to her first son and she named him James.*

# My Sister, Her Husband and His Boyfriend

My name is Lornia Cabb. I live in Kentucky. No, I'm not an ugly girl, but my sister was. She is not here to tell her story, so I have to. See she is absolutely beautiful, only he made her think she was ugly. He used to beat her ass like he was her daddy. She spent countless days locked in the house hiding bruises, cuts, and welts from the family. Who could interfere? This was what she wanted. So no one could change her mind. That "thang" she was in love with was a real piece of work. He would lie without conscience and con anybody he met. That's how he got his hook into her. She believed the lies. I really don't think it was that she was in love. I think she felt sorry for him. "That's my man!" she would say and then she would tell us to stay the hell out of her business. She followed him around like a lost puppy. She would hold his hand like they were new lovers. I can't help but think that there was something missing in her life that made her look to that trash. What is it that would make her cleave to an obvious jerk like that? See our parents had real money. They owned a horse farm and made lots of money on the derby. We never had to want for anything. My sister had been winning beauty pageants since she was 3 years old and even had a full scholarship to college, but she gave it all up for this nobody. She needed him to breathe. This asshole sold dope, she wasn't an addict. So whatever this hold was he had on her, I can't see. Abusive, criminal, and oh yeah did I mention he was bi-sexual. What good was he at all? I feel sorry for the woman who doesn't want a dick and even more so for the man who can't be satisfied with pussy alone.

I know a few of his dirty little secrets, because the guy he is screwing, just happens to live down stairs in my apartment community. I don't tell her about the all night orgies or the mid-day rendezvous that happens just a few hundred feet below me. She wouldn't believe me anyway. He tells her that he had a "deal" going down in another town or he has a lunch run to make. If you ask me, the only gangster LaTrell has in him is Sleezy, his man-friend that lives below. That also happens to be his boss. This rump wrangler is known for his switch hitting. This joker used to be married, but his wife caught him banging out a fiend with no glove and she left his ass. All the rumors and finger pointing became too much for her to bear, so she divorced him and took her kids to another state. She was smart...my sister wasn't. She also came home an hour early to surprise him and did just that. She caught them in the weirdest way you could imagine. At first, she thought Sleezy was getting on some big woman and decided to back out of the room until she heard his tired ass come lines in a falsetto voice. She shrieked and they both looked her way without even stopping. There was her boyfriend in a black and red corset, garter belt and heels getting his ass tore up! They didn't even stop pumping when they saw her in the door. She said she just stood there with her jaw on the floor, and her old man in the mix. I would have shot both those freaky bastards. That would have been one nut that they would not have gotten. She stayed. She admitted that she was a little intrigued. Sleezy eventually convinced her to join them. She said she would join that twisted world of theirs every chance they let her. I know she didn't like it. She would just sit and glare at them when they would be off talking business. Her heart would drop every time she would hear his ringtone. This is just one of the things she did to keep him happy. She would steal, she slept with other men and she would even lie to the police to keep this bastard out of trouble. Without warning, Sleezy started to fall in love with her. Why wouldn't he? She is beautiful, talented and from the screams I would hear downstairs, she was a muthafucker in the bed! Their last tryst took place on Halloween. They were having a party. All the hopheads and fiends came out to play. Sleezy went all out keeping the old and bringing in some new clients. After the festivities, they went into the usual grind. New money always seemed to turn Sleezy on, so he got as busy as he could get. What Trelle didn't know was Sleey and my sister had been seeing each other on the side for about 2 months. Sleezy stopped seeing all his other women and was planning to marry her. She knew that his getting serious about her would make bad blood between him and Trell. Sleezy knew how attached she had been to Trell, so he told her that he had made arrangements to take care of him when the time came. Sleezy had control of his business. He had fiends doing everything from stealing to killing, so he wouldn't even get his hands dirty. They would meet sometimes at my house when I was at work and Trell was at the trap. Somehow Trell got the word that his time was almost up, so he planned his last rendezvous. When I saw him that evening, he was higher than high. He said to me, "You don't want to miss the show so come down about 2:30." I must admit that I dabble a little with the pipe, so I figured I would come down and get in a little charge before the dawn. I was on my way to the apartment when I heard he all too familiar groaning. They must have really been into it because their door was cracked when I pushed on it, it just fell open.

"Hello?" I yelled to what seemed to be an empty apartment.

There were some works and a still smoking candle on the coffee table in the living room.

"Hey in here!" I ease a bit further into his place.

I saw a pipe, so I picked it up and took a hit. There went the all familiar rush. Every vein in my body felt like electricity was flowing thru it. I hit it again. Sweet.

"Oh God,...uhn..uhnh huhn..." I took one last hit and headed towards the sounds. I wandered down the hall to the 2nd bedroom. The door was standing wide open. What I saw would make a sane person scream. There was Trell fucking my sister while Sleezy was fucking him in the ass. I thought it was the blow at first. She had her eyes closed, but when she opened them I knew that they had used those works on her. She was high. My heart dropped. I guess if you knew your man was into other men it would make you want to escape too.

"Oh damn...fuck me nigga!" That was Trell's tired ass. Nasty bastard! The three of them kept grinding as if this were their last time. Then I saw Trell pull a mace out from under a jostled blanket. Yes an actual mace, you know those spiked balls on a chain that were used in medieval times. Yeah, if I hadn't see it with my own eyes, I would think it was me hallucinating too. While he was fucking my sister, he swung that thing and hit Sleezy in the head. This knocked him backward. I saw the blood gush from the wound in his head. Cookie sat up screaming. Trell started to sing a nursery rhyme as he continued to beat Sleezy to a bloody pulp. He then pulled a knife from the night stand and continued singing this whimsical dirge..

The dealer took my wife, the dealer took my wife
Hi-ho, the dairy ho...

...then he laughs a wicked laugh. One that made my blood curdle. He swings it as if to miss her on purpose. She tries to scoot away from him, but she is too out of it. He stabs her leg she cries out in pain. I run to the kitchen to grab something to hit this muthafucka with. She screamed again. There was nothing that I could do any damage with in there so I ran back to the closet in the 1st bedroom where there were a set of golf clubs. I grabbed a nine iron. I tiptoed back down the hall towards that den of sin. As I approached I noticed it had gotten quiet. The door was standing open, but not in the same position that I left it in. I called Cookie's name. She didn't answer. My stomach dropped and I could feel the bile rising to the back of my throat. I pushed the door open as far as it would go. Then I saw her laying there in a pool of her own blood. Her throat had been cut from ear to ear. Her eyes opened, and she started to reach up. I didn't see him standing behind me. Her hand drops and I begin to wail. That's when that faggot grabbed me by the throat. He started choking me. The whole time he was strangling me he told me he knew I was responsible for this. It's my fault he had to kill them. He said that he knew I had been letting them meet at my house and lying for them. As I was struggling to breathe I saw the knife he had dropped by Cookie's side. I picked it up and stabbed him in the stomach this made him release me. I bolted for the door. He pulled a gun out of nowhere and shot at me. He missed. I ran out the door. Before I could make it to the bottom of the stairs, he shot again. This time he hit me in the shoulder, I stumble but don't fall. I bang on Ms. Nelson's door and then I remembered she went to Texas to see her son. I ran out to the parking lot. I usually keep my keys in the car over the driver's side sun visor. I have two or three sets because I was always misplacing them. The door was locked. I fish around in my pocket for my house keys. Damnit! I dropped them when I slipped on the steps. I ease up to see where he was. When I stood up behind my car, there was Trell. He was covered in Sleezy and Cookie's blood. He coughs up some of his own. He then aims the gun at my head and fires.

RRRRRRRRRRRRIIIIIIIIIINNNNNNNNGGGGGGGGG!
I sit up. Damn alarm clock. It was only 7am. I had to remember to reset this thing. As I crawl out of the bed, scratching the ashy spot on my left

knee, I think of the dream I just had. This was not the first time I had this premonition. I had been seeing this event every since Cookie started seeing Sleezy behind Trell's back. As I sit on the toilet, I hear a knock on the door. They are banging on it like somebody's getting robbed.

"Alright goddammnit!" I yelled. I hate uninvited guests more than getting up early for no good reason.

As I approached the bolted door I ask, "Who is it?"

"Lornia! It's me, Cookie. Hurry and open up the door bitch! I got something to show you." She sounded so excited.

I open up the door and there she is, grinning like a Cheshire cat and waving around that 3 karat ring Sleezy gave her. My stomach dropped. I knew it was time to have the hardest talk with my sister that I had ever had.

# Date with a Rapist

Doggone it,....now Ima' be late! I spent too long under that dryer. Knowing Dinga, she probably made me late knowing I would have to pay a fine.

Dinga was one of the three other females that I lived with. She just moved here from Kansas City. Sharon, TC, herself and me all shared a 4 bedroom house out in the suburbs. This was common practice for the people in my church to share living quarters. We are all from different places in the US. Although, we all suspect that TC is from some island or maybe even Africa. She would speak with some type of gibberish when she got angry, and was always cooking something strange like cow foot, goat, or some type of animal organ that would stink up the house to no end. Sharon and myself were from San Diego I met her at a Christmas party in our office. She came over and introduced herself to me when she realized that we were the only two sober people left standing. She invited me to her church, and we became fast friends from then on. After about six years into this friendship, she bought a house and asked if I wanted to be one of her roommates. I happily accepted. Sharon was a minister in training so she allowed TC to move in on request of the pastor. Dinga was my bright idea. I knew her back in college. She appeared to be a nice girl. She was the dorm's resident beautician and she could hook up some hair. You never really know someone until you live with them. When she wrote me a letter asking if she could come for a visit because she and her mother was fighting all the time, and she needed to get away, I insisted that she stay, after all that is what we do. I saw another recruit for the church. I even went so far as to ask my boss to to hire her. Big mistake. That woman caused me all kinds of headaches. She was jealous of me for some reason and she started undermining me at every turn. She would talk crazy to my boss about our living arrangement and the curch, she would even flirt with my dates right under my nose. This hair thing was just another way to sabotage my dealings in the church.

...5:35...dang it! I reached in my purse and grabbed the 934 bus schedule. I scroll around the page looking for the Saturday schedule, and I see this bus is 6 minutes late. Shoot knowing MTS, it probably came early. That means I have to wait another hour for the next bus. I'll be way late. As I was tucking away the schedule, I notice this burgundy Camry at the light. The windows were tinted really dark, and I could hear the music thumping from the outside. As the light changed, the Camry hesitated until the car horn behind it nudged it along. It was probably my hair do. Dinga had her faults, but that girl could hook up some hair. It was finger waved across the top and had the deep waved crimps flowing down the back. I admit that getting my hair done was the one thing that I kept going for myself I didn't' have much else. See I have a cleft lip, and keeping a whipped hair do was my way of deflecting the attention from my scarred face. I was not born this way. When I was little, I bit into an electrical cord. Needless to say it charred my top lip and right cheek beyond recognition. I could have been killed but GOD spared me and left this behind as a testimony of his grace. People cringe when I say that. I just know that their thinking why couldn't HE just spare you? Did he have to leave you disfigured? I believe that if there was no scar, I probably would not have the relationship with him that I have. Not bragging, but other than these scars, I am a beautiful woman. I have the perfect little hour glass figure, hazel eyes, and smooth black skin the color of a Hershey bar. I could easily be a 10. It is painful sometimes to see the reaction of people. During my teen years I sometimes wished he had taken me to glory. Now I am in a good place with my appearance. I also had a very pleasant voice. When I sang, people forgot about my two faces. I was normal when I sang, but when the song was over so was the fantasy. They started to treat me like a monster again. Dating was very painful. Most of the guys I met were phone setups. Every now and again I would meet one who thought he could get past the scarring. He would date me for a while, get to know the real me, fall in love and declare his undying devotion to me...until, I meet his mother or sisters. Then we would only go out at night, and even then to the movies. The calls get later and later; if he even called at all. Before you know it I have been exed completely out. This has been happening to me for years. I really needed someone to call my own. In fact, I was so desperate for male attention that I would have taken anyone.

I look at my watch. Ten til six. I know I'm gonna get fined. Maybe if I just took a cab there...beep, beep. I look up. It's the Camry from before. The passenger side window rolls down, "Hey baby. You need a ride?"

"No thank you." We had been warned time and time again not to accept rides from strangers.

"You sure, you know the next bus won't be here for another hour or so."

I looked down at my watch again. If I stood out here another hour I will miss my connection and that will put me about 2 hours late for rehearsal. If that is the case, I might as well not even go.

So against everything I have been taught about strangers, I get into his car.

"My name Greg. Whatcho' name is?" He leaned in closer to me, pulling up the median.

I was hesistant to answer. I swallow my fear and say sweetly "Selenas."

"Well Selenas where you goin?" He offered a half smile as he shifted in the driver's seat.

"To choir rehearsal." The light changed, and he rounded the next corner that headed to the 5.

He put his hand on my knee and started to slowly stroke it. "I think you real pretty. I like yo' hair. Who did it?"

I swallow real hard and lightly clear my throat, "My roommate." I was starting to sweat. I shifted in my seat.

"She hooked that up." He then leaned back on the door. I could feel his eyes roaming all over my body.

I interrupted him, " You can take the 5 to Wigumm street and make a left,...Uh Greg...you can..." I paused because he passed the exit ramp. I got a cramp in my stomach.

"Uh Greg, you passed the exit ramp...Greg?" He stared straight ahead. My palms started to sweat, and my heart started to race. I called his name once again, and he totally ignored me. We turned down a side street that led to an alley way, he then turned to me with the most sinister scowl I had ever seen and said, " I know where we goin', I just wanna get me some pussy first!"

I nearly jumped out of my skin, but I played it cool so as not to get him upset. I chuckled and said, "Oh no homey, I'm already late, we gotta do this some other time!"

He looked at me with a stare so cold the hair stood up on my arms. "Bitch you thank, I'm playin' with you?" He started pawing at my thighs. I flinched and drew back. I wanted to scream, but the alley where we were parked was in back of an apartment that held mostly Hispanics. And I know that we were in gang territory, taking my chances with Greg may have been the lesser of two evils. It was almost like her was reading my mind because he put the car in gear and drove a little further down the way. I thought about jumping from the car, but when I started to reach for the door panel, he hit the power lock, and I was trapped. Once again I started to negotiate with him.

"Please, I have to go to rehearsal. We have to do this another time." He drove to what appeared to be an abandoned construction lot. I looked to the left and there was my subdivision. I put on a sweet voice and I touched his hand, "Greg please…I live right over there in Trace Lake homes. Please we can do this another time. Let me out and we will do this on another day. I…"

"Shut up bitch! Who you thank you fooling?" He proceeded to tear my blouse and grabbed my breasts, pushed them together and began to gnaw on me like I was an old chew toy. I must admit this turned me on. I wanted to go, but this rush made me want him. I pleaded again. I then explained to him that I lived right over the hill, and if he let me go I would let him come to my house. He looked me square in the eyes and dropped his hands.

"Ho, if you lying to me, I will come back here and kill you!" If I were lying to him what could he do about it? Oddly enough, I wasn't. I told him my house number. I had lost control. What in sam hill was I thinking? I just told this rapist where I lived, and I could have told him anything. Was I so desperate for male attention that I would invite someone who probably could have killed me after he finished with me, to my house. Oh my GOD!

He hit the power locks, and I hurriedly got out. As I was exiting his car, he grabbed my arm twisted, and said, "You better not be lying to me." I cupped the strap from my purse to me and ran over the hill to the backside of my suburb. As I hurried along the ivy covered fence toward the entrance, I looked toward the cul de sac and there was that burgundy Camry. I dropped my head and ran inside my house. He sped off as if he were mad. I changed clothes and called a ride to rehearsal. I made it! The whole time I was there my mind flashed back and I felt pangs of embarrassment. Why did I invite this trouble into my life? Was I completely crazy or was I secretly hoping he would come and do to me as he planned.

Sunday passed and I had pretty much forgotten about that date I made with a rapist. He probably thinks I will have the police waiting on him when he came back. Come to think of it, why haven't I told anyone about this incident? Could it be that I am ashamed of getting in a complete strangers car, after being warned so many times about doing so?

Tuesday morning, I figured the whole thing was forgotten until I walked out the door to take out the trash. I heard tires screeching and as I turned to walk back up our driveway, there was the burgundy camry. He swung open his door and simultaneously put the car in gear. I was in shock and could not think clearly. The garage door was open and the front end of his car kept me from closing it. He was on me so quick I didn't have time to catch my second breath. He pulled up one half of his t-shirt and showed me the butt end of a gun and pointed his head in the direction of the house. I knew what he was saying. I was terrified and at the same time, I was tuned on by his bravado.

When I entered the kitchen he slammed the door and bolted the locks. I stopped to turn to him, and he pushed me forward, taking the gun out his pants. When I entered the living room, he grabbed me by the back of my shorts and ripped them off. Before I could steady myself on the back of the sofa, he had his pants unzipped and was shoving his penis into my dry vagina. I cried out in pain, but this only seemed to entice him. As he continued to invade my body, a surge of pleasure hit me in my womanhood and I released a moan of shear ecstasy. I had never felt like that before, and I liked what he was doing to me. My body surrendered to the violent thrusting and I became soaking wet. This seemed to anger him, because he wanted protest. So he snatched out of me and then threw me on the floor. Then he dove on me; spreading my legs with his knee, and then proceeded to penetrate my butt. I cannot explain the pain I felt as he tore my body a second time. The whimpers of pleasure turned into cries of panic and pain. As he shoved my head to the floor and pounded me, I thought I was going to die. He grabbed my hair and pulled my head back. I could feel it ripping from my scalp. He drove me for what seemed like hours. Then just like that he jumped up and ran to the bathroom. I heard the water running so I thought he was going to clean himself. I tried to stand and gather what was left of my dignity. As I was bending over to pick up my ripped shorts, when he busted out of the bathroom and slammed his damp butt into my face. That jerk went to take a dump and used me as toilet paper. Soiled with not just emotional vile, but now I am covered in my blood, his semen and poop. If all that wasn't enough, he washed me off with his piss. After he finished, I saw him reach for his pants. I just sat there and began to cry, because I knew that he was looking for that gun to finish the job.....but get this, he cupped my head in his hand and kissed my dookey stained face and told me he liked me, so he wasn't going to kill me he was only getting his cell phone to program my number so we could go to the movies or something. He called; we went out, and eventually we got married. Now he rapes me every night.

# Ode to the "DL" Brotha

How do you hide an elephant? The
easy answer is camouflage.
But no matter what you hide it in, his
character will betray the mirage.

You can drape it in daisies, on
a backdrop so blue.
But that joker's trunk and tail will
soon be wriggling at you.

You can make it look all woodsy with
leaves of brown and green.
Just like the orange sun ablaze,
its skin can still be seen.

You can paint it white just like a
page all gussied up with words.
Yet like a train whistling in the distance,
its bleat can still be heard.

Put it in the desert, the same color as the sand.
Go to greet it with open arms, he'll
give you a hoof not a hand.

You can put him just about anywhere,
any place you could ever want,
But an elephant is an elephant is
an elephant is an elephant!

II

In time, I have found that when looking
for what you already have, you run head
long into what you can't ever possess.
This can be a car, a home, and a pair
of shoes or even a brand new dress.

Just look at you standing there in your entire
bewildered splendor. Thinking about this new
man you've found. Girl you know he's confused
about whether he has hold of the right gender.

He brags to his boys about this new 'thang' that
he has in his grasp. How he's turned her inside

and out. How he makes her sing his name. How he's tied her up and ate her like his dinner.

He'll even call her up so they can hear her voice so sweet. He'll talk about her coal black hair, her soft lips, and also her pretty feet.

All the while he's talking, seems like he bragging a bit too much for me. I mean look at this fool! How he strutting around, even Ray Charles could see!

He is so bold, so cunning, so quick to blow a kiss and tell. My sisters wake up! This brotha will fuck a snake if someone would hold the tail.

Speaking of tails, you better watch yours. Cause he's eyeing you and will probably be knocking down your doors. But you hold fast and take these I give to you. Don't let that rascal in. He's just after you cause you new.

Watch the smooth way he works his way into your life. That scoundrel will even tell you he wants you to be his wife.

But alas I warn you to look at him with a frown. As soon as he gets wind of new meat, he will also put you down.

My sister be brave, because what he got

he should sell it. That's the best dick in this
town, and let me be the one to tell it!

Just remember it comes with a warning label
and a long line of symptoms I am given.
This brother is not the driver, but
this nigga likes to get driven!

# Loving me some Miserable

"Thank you ma'am." I dropped my head and walked away from her desk. This is the third no I have heard since I left the office. I just got to get some money. I am $120.00 short on the rent. I had it all. I just spent it on him. I know that I should have paid it two days ago, but he needed some shaving clippers, some cologne and some new underwear. I had to buy us some groceries didn't I? I mean I had to treat him better than all those other women he has had. I got to make him love me. This is the only way.

**"I'm in love..."**

Beyonce's Dangerously in Love was the ring tone I had set for him.

"Hey baby" Talking to him always put a smile on my face.

29

"What you doing?"

"I'm trying to get us some money."

"Some money...from where?"

"From a cash advance place." I knew he was gonna be mad that I spent rent money on him.

"From a cash advance place?" He sighs heavily. I'm hoping he doesn't ask me why. Right now I really don't feel like lying to him. "Why?"

"Because you still need stuff."

He sighs heavily. "Don't worry about me, I'm fine."

"But baby, I want you to be ok." I worried about him soo much.

"I am ok! What you cooking tonight?"

"Same thing I cook every night Pinky,...chicken and rice." With the budget I got to feed a two person household on, he's lucky there is something to cook.

He Heaves another heavy sigh. I was going to surprise him with his favorite cut of steak and twice baked potato if I had gotten that loan.

"Baby I broke my sunglasses again. You got $20 so I can get some more?"

"Yeah baby I got you." We are already $120 in the hole, what's twenty more dollars.

He interrupted my thoughts. "Where are you now?"

"I'm almost at the apartment." I needed to run home and grab a pair of pantyhose. The ones I was wearing had more holes than a pair of finshnets.

"I'm at a board meeting. I just stepped out to grab some water from the fridge. I'm running low you better put that on your shopping list. Before you come back to the office, why don't you stop at the mall and grab me another pair. Oh yeah, while you're out, stop at Hunan's and get me some of that pepper steak I love, we are about to break for lunch and my stomach growling like a grizzly."

"Okay baby. I will see you in a few minutes. I love...(click).." He was probably having trouble with his cell phone. It always hung up at the oddest moments.

I stop at East Lake Mall. Hunan's is in the same complex so I can stop after I leave Lenzez. I could stop at Rollers on the way home and get the waters tonight. I would do anything to please him. He has had a rough life. For starters, he grew up in the system. He was displaced after he accidently shot his brother and his mother hung herself. He went to live with his biological father, but this guy made Hitler look like a saint. Between the underserved beatings with electrical cords, cable wires, and an occasional brick to the back of the head, he was also subject to the nonsensical ramblings about how his mother was a whore and he could be anybodies kid. He had often talked about the closet time. This was where he was made to wear girl's panties and perform felatio on his father. As he was telling me these things, tears would form in his eyes, and I knew it did not just stop there. Fate was forth telling when he was given the name Miserable.

His mother GOD rest her soul, named him for a time in her painful life when she found out that she was pregnant with the child of a man who could care less about her. He used to beat her unconscious, knowing that she had an inoperable brain tumor. He would often talk about how his dad would slam her head into the closet door, or drag her down the stairs. He told me once that he had sneaked a knife out of the kitchen and had crept up the stairs while that drunken fool was sleeping. Just before he planted it in his father's chest, the hand of his sickly mother touched his shoulder, and told him to let it go. His father awoke suddenly to see Miz standing over him with the knife and pulled out his pistol. "Boy you thank you grown! Ima send yo' blalck ass straight to hell!" and he shot at Miz. Not long after that he and his brother found that gun and were playing gangsters in the front yard when Miz accidently shot Maynard. They were just playing. Miz didn't know that the gun was loaded. The boy lived for 42 hours and then he died. Miz's mom was so heartbroken, that she hanged herself from the shower rod. Miz blamed himself and then he became angry with her. Why did she leave him knowing he had no one else in the world? He wished that he too were dead. He wanted to be out of pain too. All he knew was he was left behind. Left in the hands of this tyrant they called his daddy. What a life to have lived. Everything I could do in my power to make him feel whole again, I was going to do. If it meant being behind on my rent, or letting my car insurance go, whatever he needed I was going to make it right. After all he just broke off his 3rd marriage. Before he came to live with me, he left yet another woman and to top all of that off, he just got out of jail...again. It is just a streak of bad luck. It will get better for him. I spent most mornings crying and praying to GOD that he would change him and make him okay. I had an incident where I ran off the road because I was crying so hard over him. He had spent the night with his little girl... that reminds me, I got to get her something, her birthday is coming up. Her mother is tripping. She had him locked up because he was six months behind in his child support. That was just wrong. He was a little behind, but I was catching him up. Anything I could do was no problem.

I pull into the mall parking lot, getting ready to enter in the Macy's side to get the Lenzez outlet, it's Miz.

"Yes my baby!" I just loved to do things for him.

"Don't worry about getting me lunch."

"But bae, I already got it! I..." He interrupted me.

"Just put it in the fridge, and I will eat it later. Listen, if I'm not in my office when you get back, just wait until this afternoon to bring those glasses. They called a special session and I will be humping for the rest of the afternoon." I thought I heard a man giggle in the background.

"What time do you think you will be back here?" he asked.

"I just got one more stop and I will be there. What do you need?" I was so disappointed. I really wanted to see him before I went back to work.

"Never mind just take your time. I will talk to you later. I got this session to get to. I am going to skip lunch all together." Then I heard the dial tone.

He is always doing something. I wish I could settle his mind. He barely sleeps and when he does drift off, he jumps at the slightest movement.

After two grueling hours I drag myself back into the office. As I am heading towards the elevators I think I see Miz getting on. I rush to beat the doors, and to my surprise, it is him and his friend Lewis and I see he has a Train Track sub in his hand. He probably ran out to get it before he had to get back to the office. That is so like my baby. He is too busy to pay attention to what's right in front of his face. I smile knowingly at him, and he turns away. That's normal. Our affair is supposed to be a secret.

We have known each other for about 12 years, and had been seeing each other off and on for most of that time. It was mostly when he was between marriages or he just needed to get away from any one of his 3 ex-wives. At the time we met, I was married. My husband was no match for Miz in the bedroom, so I chose to leave the confines of my convenient relationship for the uncertainty of being the other woman. After he passed me over for the second time, I moved back to Arkansas for the last three of the twelve years I had know him to care for my mother. When she died, Nettlesville was not big enough for me anymore. So I made my way back to Vegas where I got a job for Xandrum, Powers and Ressing law firm as a paralegal. Turns out, Miz had just been named head officer in their labor law department. When I started there, he was on a medical leave of absence. We started seeing each other again after he got out of the hospital. I made the mistake of telling this blabbermouth sissy named Seth, and before you know it, we are water cooler gossip. At first he acted like he didn't know who I was because he had made this connection with a chick named Jessica, but I wasn't having that. I had already been thru too much with him for some other skank to jump in and claim what I thought was mine. I can see his jaw clenching. Poor thing that tooth is probably bothering him again. Which reminds me; I need to make him a dentist appointment so that he can get that cracked molar filled.

The elevator doors open to the 5th floor and they get off. He turns just as the doors close and shoots me a wink. I smile and think to myself how lucky I am.

"Ms. Mickey, aren't we a little early for tomorrow. Oh I'm sorry; you are back from your lunch hour 2 hours late! You been gone so long I thought you had called it a day!" That was my oaf of a manager Mr. Petit.

"No sir Mr. Petit" I answered, putting on a fake smile. "I had some errands that ran long, and ..."

"Save it! Stop by my desk on your way out." He turned that meatloaf shaped body of his around and tried to waddle away.

"Yes sir." Fat muthafucker. I hate that man, or woman, or whatever he is this week. A friend of mine who just happens to be gay has seen him in drag hanging out on Sunset Boulevard picking up men. He pimps himself out like a cheap slut. That's not the first time I had heard he was into men. Someone else told me that the only reason he has so many words for me is because he had this thing for Miz. I can see jealousy in a lot of the things he says, like he is always putting down my hairstyles, and trying to call me out and make fun in some form of my attire or my skin color.

I am clearing some files from my desk, when I get the message that there is a package for me downstairs at the security desk. I put the stamp on the final two, and then put them in interoffice envelopes. I glance up and see Jessica, Miz's other woman, leaving her desk as well. I stop at Clara's desk and thank her for the cheesecake she brought to my luncheon on Tuesday. I get on the elevator and as soon as the doors closed

I shift my pantyhose. That's the last time I wear these control tops, shit, let my ass jiggle all it wants! The elevator doors open on the 2nd floor. To my surprise… it's Miz and that skank Jessica! I quickly look away and pretend that I don't see either one of them. I make it a point to ignore her when he is around. I want to show him that I am mature and that I am allowing him space to set things right so we can be together.

"Humph." She makes it a point to roll her eyes and grunt as if I had been following them. He puts his hand in the small of her back and clears his throat as if to change the subject. What this bitch doesn't know is that every time he exhales that's my pussy on his breathe. He was moaning and grinding in my wetness this morning before his shower. Who the fuck does she think she is? The doors open and before they get off, he whispers something to her and they both laugh. I am weak. Every time I see those two together it's like a kick in the stomach. My heart is in so many pieces now I can hardly walk, but I do what I have always done when it comes to him. I walk up to the desk and Rico greets me.

"Hey my beautiful black sistah!" He always made a fuss over me. This was one of those mornings that his advances were welcome.

"Hey Rick. Is there a package for me?" I give him a smile to promise him something he will never get.

"Sure thing. Just sign your name right here, and

put your phone number right here." He flashes his gold toothed smile.

"My number?" I pretend to be aloof. He does this at least twice a week.

"Yeah baby, you sign here for the package, and put your number here so I can call you for a date." I smile. He was so kind to me. Why hadn't I given him a chance?

'I am in love with you'

It was that damned message tone again. I quickly press he ignore button. Just what the fuck am I wasting my time with that punk for? I am too good to him for him to treat me the way he does. It's one thing to be messing around, but to treat me like trash is another.

### 'I am in love with you'

Just what the fuck does he want to tell me? How she bumped into him on the elevator and she was about to fall that's why his hand was in the small of her back. My message tone beeps.

'you kno I love you...she just a friend'

I was so relieved. Maybe he is trying to find a way to break it off. It's not easy and I did tell him I would be patient. It had only been a month since everything happened and I could wait forever to be with him. Things are always so complicated for him. I make my way back up to my desk. Here comes fat ass like clockwork. "You just determined not to work today ain't you honey." I totally ignore him. My message tone beeps again.

'will be home late got some
meetings running late'

Good that will give me time to get those waters and finish cooking.

My landlord is such a schmuck. This is the third time this week he has been in my apartment when I wasn't home. All he is doing is seeing if I had vacated before he got his money. I ain't moving just late on the rent. I clean and season the chicken, put it in the streamer and start the rice cooker. I put the still frozen Brussel sprouts in a small boiler with some butter, salt, and a little water. I walk by the freezer once more to pull those chitterlings out. Miz loves those. I will probably cook these for him with some collards on Sunday. The timer on the steamer and rice cooker go off and I turn the gas off under the sprouts. My message beeps:

'baby get my plate ready, I'm on my way'

I set his place at the table and put some ice in a glass. I won't fix his plate just yet. He likes to takes a shower and lay out his clothes for the next day before he eats. I hear a siren in the distance. I think nothing of it because the hospital is not too far away. I prepare the plate but I cover it and place it in the microwave that way when he is in the shower I can zap it for a few minutes. I will go through the mail while I wait for my beloved Miz to arrive.

I look over at the clock on the cable box it says 11:43. Where the hell is he? I get up and start towards the bedroom. I text him. I just want him to know that I know what he's up to, so I send him a message saying save me some and your plate is in the microwave.

As I am changing into my wool pj's because it ain't no way he getting none after being almost 4 hours late, the phone rings. I'm mad as hell so I flip open my phone and yell "Just what the fuck is it you trying to prove? Where you at?"

"Ma'am. This is Officer Jackson with the Las Vegas police department. Are you familiar with a Mizerable Stevens?"

Oh lord! Another one of those warrants has probably caught up with his ass. "Yes, what's the problem officer?" My stomach dropped. All I have is the rent money. I can't afford bail right now.

"Well it seems that Mr. Stevens has been shot."

I dropped the phone.

# AFTER CARE

I rush to open the door. Miz has been in therapy for the past six months. It was touch and go there for a minute. The bullet is still in his spine, but he is learning to walk and use his right hand again. He has been in a funk for three days. He always gets like this when they tell him he going to be in therapy for another three months. He feels like I am holding him back; that he can't heal properly when he's here with me. I cook him three meals a day, I bathe him, and I feed him I even wipe his ass when he shits. Even though he is sitting in wheel chair, I keep his jeans starched to crisp, his sneakers white, his finger and toe nails clipped and clean and his hair cut. His disability check is only about 455 after his daughter's mother takes her cut. She also gets the food stamps to cover what the check doesn't. Since I am not his wife it is taking a long time for them to decide to give me a guardian's check. Notwithstanding, I have been taking care of him since he got shot. I do it all in hope that he will see how much I love him, how much he means to me.

"Bae...I'm fixing some meat loaf and cabbage for you is that ok?" he just sits there and scowls. I begin to cook.

"Would you like to watch some television?"

I look at him and he is just staring at me like his eyes could burn a hole through me. I turn on the tv on and scroll through the listings and see that they have one of those marathons of those crudely drawn Japanese cartoons. He loves that Inuyasha. I turn it up so he could hear it.

"Would you like something to drink?" I don't wait for him to answer. I have been doing everything else for him, so I gauge when he's hungry, when he's tired, even when he's thirsty. I hope he sees how much I think about him and realize what he has. I pour him a glass of mountain dew. I add some ice and put a straw in it. I reach into the pantry to get his tray. I think he might want a snack so I grab a bag of chips from the middle shelf. As I am setting this up, he moans for me. He can't say my name completely yet, but I know when he is trying to tell me something. He motions for me to come to him with his left hand. I lean in and that joker smacks me across my cheek. May be he is still grouchy. I continue to set up the tray and just as I turn to walk away, he pushes everything to the floor. I continue walking towards the kitchen. He does this twice a week. He starts to cry openly. I am at my wits end. My tears flow as well. He's miserable and there is nothing I can do about it.

"G'morning lovely lady!" Rick was at it again.

"Hi." I was really in no mood to entertain his particular brand of country.

"Baby everything ok?" I had no right to be angry at him. After all he was the only one who was still civil to me. After that sissy Seth spilled the beans about me and Miz's affair, slowly but surely everyone started to choose sides. Unfortunately, none of them was on my side. I want so desperately to yell, hell no! I am doing all I can for a man who could care less. I know that he doesn't give a good goddamn about me, but I am the only one he has. His sisters wanted nothing to do with him. All the bitches he been humping around with suddenly found themselves with other priorities. Even the ho he took that bullet for went back to her husband. She had five kids and one was on the way. Rumor had it that it was his. Now I'm the one stuck with his ass.

I fake a smile and tell yet another lie. "oh everything is wonderful and you?"

"Still waiting on you to let me take you out." I smile. His eyes caught mine and for the first time I see compassion in them. Tears began to flow and I turn and run towards the elevator. As the doors proceed to close, suddenly they are stopped. It was the guard. He puts his hand on my shoulder and attempts to comfort me. For the first time in almost a year someone was attending to my needs, and it felt damn good. I lean in to the crook of his shoulder. He squeezes me close to him and then the bottom falls out. He pushes the stop button on the elevator. I get a hold of myself.

"I…I am sorry." I wipe my teary eyes.

He said, "Baby it's ok. I know what you have been going through."

I pull back and look in his face. He begins to tell me how the entire building is talking about me Miz, and what a fool I have been. I thought those stares were of envy. I would see people whispering when I walked by, but I didn't know I was the talk of the office. I continue to straighten up and ask him, "What exactly are they saying?"

"Well it turns out your boy had been very busy…and not just with women either." He looks at me with this sheepish grin on his face. I felt my stomach rising to the back of my throat.

"Please Rick, spare me the details." I tried to

turn and walk away. I have been feeling dizzy all morning. Besides I have had this migraine for the past two days.

"Naw baby, I ain't trying to make you feel any worse. You got a shoulder to cry on any time." He said leaning into me.

With that being said I smoothed my hair and try dabbing at the corners of my eyes. I look at him and proceed to speak, but I couldn't get anything out. I wanted to thank him for making me feel loved for a minute. He took my hand and gave it a knowing squeeze. The doors to the elevator open and I put on the mask.

It has been another year and Miz is up and around. I look haggard. This man is sapping all of my energy. I am happy that he is doing so well, but he is more like himself than I wanted him to be. He gave me a ring and in a month or so I will be wife number 4, but nothing has changed. I am asking myself some heavy questions and not coming up with any sound answers. I will have some time to think this weekend, because he is going off to his little girls' house this weekend. I know what that is code for. He's not talking about his daughter he is talking about Jessica. She is short, pale and kind of resembles a fruit bat. She has an hour glass figure and if she wasn't such a skank a great personality. I have had a chance to talk with her, but she was too busy playing the game to really listen. I am not the type of woman to fight another for the affection of a man. Not because I am afraid, but because he is going to love who he loves and there is nothing my involvement with the other woman will change. My mind is so full of drama that I don't' see or hear the truck flashing his lights or honking his horn. I swerve and skid. The car flips over into a ravine. I can feel the blood dripping down my neck. I don't feel much else. All I want to do is sleep. I hear someone call my name. I hear them, but I can't answer. If I could just rest my eyes for a little while.

## MY TURN...

I open my eyes. Feels like I been out for a minute. It hurts to blink. My mouth is so dry. My nose feels clogged up. I probably broke it in the accident. I try to speak, but my throat is also full and dry. Suddenly a nurse appears. She is running back and forth. I hear her talking but I can't understand her. Then there is a doctor over my head. He checks my eyes with his pen light. I want to sit up but I can't because my legs feel so heavy. I try to speak, but the nurse pats my shoulder and tells me to just hang on. I wonder how long I've been out. It kind of feels like I have to pee. May be I can go the bathroom. I hope they don't make me sit on one of those bed pans. I reach for the nurse and she takes my hand. I smack my lips and try to say that I am thirsty. She gauges my responses and puts these lemon flavors q-tips in my mouth. By my face must be in bad shape. I put my hand on my nose to see how much damage had been done and that's when I feel it. There is a tube in my nose. I start to panic. The nurse sees me and then she grabs my and. She puts this cuff on it. I try once again to touch my face but my hand is stuck to my side. I moan. She comes to the bed side and rubs my shoulder. I want to ask so many questions, but I am stuck. I can't form the words. I feel the tears stroll down my cheeks. I look over and see the nurse putting a needle in the IV and then I feel this wave of calm wash over me. A slow moan creeps from my lips and can hear myself hum as I drift off into peace.

As I wake from my stupor, I feel a little sharper. Still feels like I have to pee. I have probably been out for hours. Last thing I remember was this tube running out of my nose. My neck is still kind of stiff, but I feel a tingling in my legs. I try once again to sit up. There is a beeping. Another nurse comes in. I know I have probably been out for hours. I got to call Miz and tell him about the accident. Oh yeah, I need to let fat ass know I will be out for the couple of days. He is going to eat his up. I can just hear him now' Ms. Mickey you done found another way to get out of work. This is something that can't be helped. I try to tell her that I need to go to the bathroom and then I need to find my cell phone to tell all my people that I am ok. My tongue feels so heavy. I can't form the words.

She starts examining me. I try to look and see her name tag. She's not a nurse she is a doctor. I see the light flashes and I felt the needle in my foot. I try to tell her this, but it's as if she knows. I struggle with the words; it's as if I have cotton in my mouth, but they come.

"Wh…wh…what   hh…hh…hhappen'd?"   I managed to eek out a few incoherrrent words.

"Your speech may take a little while to come back. It's hard to tell with some strokes."

Did she say stroke? Oh my God! I had a stroke! I try so hard to ask her just what the hell she means I had a stroke. She keeps talking. "You were so lucky. It turns out that your accident was not nearly as bad as it appeared. You only suffered a few cuts and scrapes. Unfortunately, while you were in the emergency room, you suffered a stroke. If you had been alone and had it, you probably would have died. We were able to contain the bleeding and kept your impairment to a minimum."

"H…hh…how…ll…lllong?"

"How long has it been?" she seemed to be reading my mind. I muster a nod.

"It's been about 3 weeks."

3 weeks!!! That's not possible. I don't have that much time to take off from work. I got to find my cell phone. What has Miz been eating? I know every towel in the house is dirty. I got to get out of here, he needs me. How is he paying the bills? Oh my poor baby. I try to ask her when I can go

home. She then becomes patronizing and tells me to save my strength because I will need it.

"You are going to need all of it to get back to normal. I will arrange for you to start therapy as soon as possible. Now all you need is the motivation to get strong again." I already had that's my Mizerable.

"Push Miss Mickey! You got to get it all back, so keep pushing!" That was my physical "terrorist", Ms. Antley. Even though she has been very supportive, I hate her. She drives me to complete exhaustion and pain, but her efforts have gotten me up and walking. I'm not at full strength, but I have come a long way.

"Ugh, I can't!" I broke down for the third time during our session. Then I thought about my tentative release date. I will get to be home with my man. I know he can't stand to see me in here. I know he would have come to see me by now, but he hates hospitals. That's ok because I will be home soon and everything will be as close to normal as I can get it.

"Ms. Mickey based on your progress these past few sessions, I have decided to let you go home a couple weeks early. You can tell your family that they can come and get you at nine am on Thursday!" I don't know who was more excited, me or Dr. Johnson. She just doesn't know, if I could stand up without this walker, I would do a cartwheel. I'm going home to my baby. I pick up the cell phone and try to call Miz. No answer. He has his phone on airplane mode when he's out and bout during the day. so I text him. Shit I should have just left him a message because it takes me so long with these buttons.

'I need you'

He calls me right back. "What's going on?" Miz has his problems, but when I use the "n" word, he will get back to me.

"I...I'm going to get to come home on Thursday morning and I need you here at 8:30." I have gotten most of my speech back. I still stutter a little.

"I can't. I have a meeting that will run me past 8:45. Why don't you see if you can get someone else to come and pick you up."

I was a little out done by his request. What could be more important than me? After all, I nurtured him back to full health without any complaint. Besides the only one who could pick me up is my sister and she lives in Colorado, and Thursday is two days away. I try to convince him that I can wait until 9:00 if he wanted me to. He reluctantly grunts out an 'alright'. I give him the rest of the details and confirm a 9:30 pickup time. An hour later Miz sends me a text back and asks me how the pussy is feeling, and if I'm going to be ready for him to beat it up. I text him back that I don't think I will be ready for all that.

I finish all of my breakfast and give myself a shower. I have been on pins and needles since about 2am. I could hardly sleep last night. I'm actually going to be in my own bed tonight.

"Well I see you are ready to put us down." Nurse Watkins was laughing so hard she had to grab the side of my bed. She began taking out the ports and the IV. She explained what the prescriptions were for and how I was supposed to take them. I look over at the clock and it was 8:32. I could feel my heart racing. I hadn't seen my Miz since before the accident. Like I said I know he would have been here he just doesn't like hospitals or sick people, and now that I'm getting out of this place we could get back to our lives. How in the world am I going to toddle down the aisle with this walker? Anyway, I can see me now. I have gained a little weight since I been in here, but nothing a few laps and a little dieting won't cure. 8:47. I call Miz to let him know I am all packed and ready to go when he gets here. No answer so I text him. I hear faint giggles and the phone starts to vibrate. That's the ringtone for my friend Jeanella. She has been the only one who has come to see me since I have been sick. She has been a true friend to me through these trying times. When I am down she calls and inspires me telling me that it's our time. You can make it because you're strong woman, and don't let the past interfere with where you are going...she has just been a rock for me. 8:52 I try to call Miz once again. No answer. I start to feel butterflies in my stomach.

\*\*\*

# Ugly

## Is as ugly does

\*\*\*

# Almost

The best day of my life turned out to be the worst day of my life. I was invited to an old friend's house to meet a very prominent business woman, who could launch my career. As I was leaving, my best friend in the whole world turned to me and said, "I think you've made it!" Lolina was connected to every outlet of entertainment in the industry. The party was a success and she wanted to see me again. Unfortunately, she had another engagement and that she was there only to collect business cards. I looked at the dainty clutch with disdain, for I knew I had left my information back in the gator covered briefcase I lug around every day. The one time I should be loaded down with my business tools, I chose to travel light. I began to stutter and sweat.

"I'm so sorry Ms Lolina! I am usually better prepared than this." I exclaimed as I searched every inch of that clutch, hoping there was a remnant left from another adventure. She stood there and looked at me with a look that was screaming what's the occasion for your incompetence today? She gave me a short nod and looked away. I knew then I had missed my opportunity to impress her. I quickly turned away to scour the crowd for anyone of the associates I thought I could count on surely one of them has my card. That was to no avail. They all looked at me as if I was speaking a foreign language. No love was in their eyes. I had finally made it though. I saw them all for who they truly were...SHARKS! Just before it bites, sharks eyes go dark and cold. His only mission in life at that point is to bite and devour. This is now the scene I am standing in, a cold dark and murky depth, where it's kill or be killed. I had made it to the back of the room when my biggest rival for this position, handed me a card with the purple logo on it. It was from my first set of business cards. I had grown since then, but the information was still valid. I rushed with all the finesse this moment afforded me only to be disappointed. Lolina was getting into the back of the airport limo and headed to heights unknown without me. I turned once again to this crowd of teeth and they were filled with smiles. The cold eyes had turned into warm and fuzzy sneers.

"So how did you do?" I wasn't sure if she was mocking me or really interested in this wasted opportunity. I felt as if I could disappear into thin air. She must have read the expression on my face, because she put her arm around me and whispered, "Nothing beats a failure but a try. If it's not this time, maybe a little further down the line." She offered a sweet smile and a gentle pat. As she walked toward the bar, I knew that she was just trying to make me feel better. I exhale in sheer disappointment. My life's work and dreams somehow had just taken a detour.

"Thank you all for coming and have a safe drive home." Lisa Tasker was the most gracious host in the entire Peach State. Making a connection with her was the best move I had ever made. Maybe one day I will be in a position professionally to thank her for all of her motivation. I gather my wrap and that career forsaking clutch. It was a rare find and already it was the bane of my existence. As soon I as get home, it's going in the trash. Once again Lisa pats me on the shoulder and gives me a reassuring look. I smile regrettably and hurry towards the door. When I reach my car, I lay my head against the steering wheel. What a fool I had been. A once in a lifetime venture and I blow it! I sit and brood for another 10 minutes and then I start the engine. Out of the corner of my eye I see Sharona Johnson, an up and coming writer grinning with all 132 of her teeth. She was one of the fortunate ones who got their business cards in the hands of Lolina. One day I'm going to be smart like them. I slowly place the car in drive and proceed to pull out of the driveway. I had to stop for a moment because I forgot how to get out of this neighborhood. I remember the directions were still in my glove box. I sort thru the old insurance cards, a flashlight and an open battery pack to my moment's treasure. I noticed that Lisa's house was at the center of her community. That was Ms Tasker all the way. She was always at the center of all things social. It's funny how fate can give us information about our destinies. I was always a day late, missing opportunities or out of place in some way. Just as that thought was leaving my head, my cell phones rings. I listened to see whose id it was. Oh shoot it was the unidentified caller tone. Usually I send those calls straight to voicemail, but something in me felt an overwhelming curiosity.

"Hello!?" I always made it a point to sound bothered by these calls. That way if it is a wrong number, they are reluctant to ever call back again.

"I'm sorry, I was calling for a Ms Rawlins is she available?" I recognized that slow smooth accent anywhere.

"Hello Lolina!" My soul felt as if it would jump out of my body.

"Ms Rawlins? Oh I am so relieved, for a minute I thought that I had the wrong number....have I caught you at a bad time?"

"No!!!" I was looking for the first spot to pull over before my heart jumped out of my chest. I tried to pull it together because destiny was calling me from an unknown number.

"No, I was just leaving the party." I tried to sound as nonchalant as my nerves would let me. My hands were shaking so much until it sounded like I was traveling thru a tunnel. I had almost sweated thru my chiffon blouse and my iphone was covered in Fashion Fair's finest foundation, but I had been waiting my whole life for this one call. Everything I had done in the genre of entertainment was coming to its peak right now. I was so enthralled in our conversation that I drove right by my exit.

"I'm so happy you called me. I was beginning to think I had lost out." I didn't want her to think I was a chuckle headed loser, so I played on her sympathy. "See..."

Before I could finish Lolina interrupted me. "Ms Rawlins..." she sighed. "This is not a very forgiving business. One slip up could terminate your whole career. You must step up and be active in your own success. No one likes a whiner or someone they have to babysit. I only give one chance. Once you let me down I will become as cold as that crowd you had to face today. It's okay to call me El...All of my associates do."

The laughter just jumped out of my throat when I heard this. "Oh El that was...." She interrupted me again.

"I just happen to be great friends with LT. She explained your situation to me and because she thinks so highly of you, I am going against my better judgment and giving you a shot. I want your first three manuscripts edited and copied on bonded paper. Have them messaged to my office at 8am tomorrow morning. I will be leaving for Amsterdam at 10 so have everything delivered by then. While I am on location I will be calling to give you some feedback on what I have read and which one I will be selecting for your first movie."

I could have shit! Did she say my first movie?

"My office address is 3990 Marcus Lane, suite 318. Please have them delivered in 3 separate envelopes so that I can keep track of each individual script. This is your one chance so don't let LT down."

"Oh wow Lolina! I won't. I will have them delivered ASAP! How can I thank you for this opportunity?" I pulled my phone back and to my surprise she had hung up. I began to panic. Had she hung up or did my stupid phone drop the call? Damn! I pondered each possibility. Perhaps she is like that devil who wore Prada and was just impatient because she didn't have to wait on anybody. People in her position didn't have to wait for anyone. She was everywhere I wanted to be. Or maybe my phone lost her as I drove under the overpass. Overpass? I don't remember that on the way here. Where the hell am I? I looked at the squalid surroundings. I wasn't in Buckhead anymore. I had crossed over into its urban equivalent. I followed this narrowing; lightless street for about two blocks suddenly there was no one around. I had never been more frightened in my life. I knew then I would be leaving here without my jewelry and possible without my 745. Why didn't I drive the Jag? It is older and paid for. I looked to the left and there were some abandoned apartments, to my right an old gas station. Straight ahead was a downhill road that narrowed into an alley. I was getting ready to scream, when this woman came running out of nowhere. She was about 5'7, 143 pounds, and she had long black hair that framed her mocha skin. She looked completely flustered. As she approached my car, she became more frazzled and began yelling frantically.

"Hurry...you have to come with me!" She screamed.

"Why? What's going on?" I was so nervous, I forgot all about Hollywood and my new connections. I thought about my attire and all of my jewelry I began to take off my rings.

"Lady there's no time for that! You have to come now. They are coming!" She started banging on the passenger side window. I was glad that she was there to help me, but this car costs 100 grand!

"Ma'am what's going on?" I scope out the territory, and I see a white tempo speeding towards us. I knew then, it was time to boogie.

"Oh shit!" I left my phone, my purse and what little jewelry I had taken off. I had on some pewter metallic mules with low heels so I could run it if I had to.

As we turned the corner and ran up hill for two blocks, the car continued to follow. The only thing I saw was a check cashing joint and a dingy grocery store. The car took a detour around the corner. We continued towards the check cashing place. It looked like a safe place, because the entire store front was Lucite. I was dog tired, but my safe haven was only a few feet away. The store owner saw us running and rushed to open the door. As I entered I noticed a faint smell of chronic… maybe this was just a front for the neighborhood street pharmacist. In any event I was glad they were helping. Just as the owner was locking the door, the couple in the white tempo sped past the door. I couldn't hear what they were saying because of the window casing, but it looked like they were trying to get my attention.

"That's odd." Not only did my mouth say it but my body felt it. I could have sworn that they were some rowdy teenagers or local gang members trying to pull a mugging for some quick cash. They were in for a treat because I think I lost my keys. "DAMNIT!!" Both the store owner and the lady look at me in the strangest way. Instead of the look of pity, they looked at me like I was a naughty child misbehaving. The lady straight way pulled me behind the second layer of glass. I never felt so safe and so confused in my life. They couple didn't look like robbers or gang members; actually they appeared to be church goers. He had on a black jacket and a collarless shirt that could have easily been a clergy collar. The woman, who was driving the car, was white. She was kind of plump with strawberry blond hair and a shit load of freckles. She stuck her head out of the window and began yelling until she turned blush red. The man was pointing some kind of journal in his hand and waving it wildly. Before I could figure it out, I could feel the cold shaft of the nine millimeter in the small of my back.

"Okay bitch...we gone play this real cool ok? Tell them its okay so they can get the fuck away from my store." My bladder was about to drop. "Now!" He then jammed the gun into my spine.

I paint on a big cheesy grin and wave them away, but the man and woman continued to shout. The woman almost got out, but the afro-Asian sister who had led me there walked toward the door. The woman backed down as if she knew she was about to catch an ass whipping. She climbed back into the car and slowly drove back down the alley where my BMW, my life and my career were stranded. The two people who were screaming at the store were ministers and that journal he was waving was the bible. Turns out this woman was a cop and she and this wrinkled old pimp were into white slavery.

After my salvation drove off, I was forced into the back room of that raggedy store and shoved onto a cot. Instinct kicked in and I began to struggle not so much to escape, but out of frustration. I wasn't going to make my deadline, my scripts weren't going to get read, no movie with my name on it will ever be made and my freedom as I knew it would become a distant memory. That old fart grabbed both my arms and pinned me down. I kneed him in the groin and kicked until I felt the needle in my neck. That was the last thing I remember from that night.

Here I am two years later worn out emotionally and physically, and with no future in sight. I often sit and try to remember some of my old numbers and acquaintenances, but nothing comes clear. Even if they were to find me, I'm not sure they would want me back. From that day to this one I have been hooked on heroin. A passion for writing used to drive me, but now it is my next fix that is my new motivation. I would awake from dreams that were so real I could smell the characters breathe. Now I awake from stupors with my sheets stained with vomit and the semen of the many men I am forced to bed. I used to smell of sweet rose petals and the fresh lilac, now I am tainted with the sweat of john's and my own piss. Who knew fate was so unkind. I often think of LT and wonder what made her so special that she escaped this hell. What had I done to deserve this kind of torture? My life was nothing like I had imagined, yet I had nothing to go back to.

# Warriors of the Night

"Go clean yourself off." He bumps me out of the bed. I walk the few feet to the toilet and I sit down. I can't believe tonight he kissed me. So what are we supposed to be a couple now? I guess if you sticking your dick in somebody on the regular you bound to catch feelings for them. This is the part I hate the blood. After the first time I leaked so much you would of thought I was a bitch on the rag. After about 10 minutes of wiping shit and blood off me, I stand or I try to stand, walk over to the make shift mirror and I catch a glimpse of what used to be a man. There are still remnants of me there, but not enough that I recognize. I look at my black eye, bruised jaw and busted lip. A feeling of nausea and regret washes over me. It could be the fact that big, burly joker just got thru juggling my intestines around or is it that I may be catching feelings for him too. He clears his throat and turns back toward the light. That was my cue. So I grab the rag off the sink and I carefully wrap his dick in the warm clothe and clean my filth and shame off his manhood.

After this ritual of passion I climb back into the bottom bunk with him. He insists that I keep him warm until the lights come up. Maybe I have been in here too long, but this is the part I secretly long for. I lay my head in the nook of his arm. This made the whole scene tolerable...being near him that is. It satisfies a longing that no woman could ever give me. I have had some quality ass in my days, but nothing quite like his. Laying here in his arms completes a search, scratches an itch, and quenches a thirst that wasn't reachable before now. But it can't continue. I can't keep denying my manhood by succumbing to his. I have got to put up a better fight.

Today I got a letter from my little girl. She drew a picture of her daddy behind bars. This breaks my heart. I have got to get out of this place so I can bring her up right. My baby is the most important thing to me. As I am deep in thought about my baby girl, _____ walks up behind me and grunts for me to go see Murddock. I sigh and quickly get to the one bathroom we have in the Rec area of Shumwa prison. This is the nastiest place on earth. There's always shit or piss in the toilet. One day somebody had spit all over the floor the walls even on the toilet seat. After the first time _____ sent me here, I caught this rash on my left leg that wouldn't heal. They ended up cutting away some skin, and muscle tissue so now there is a whole in my leg. Damn. I forgot to buy some paper down here. Two knocks on the door let me know my date was her. I flush the toilet with my foot and take a seat pants up. I was just supposed to give him head. _____ has been using me to pay his drug debts since I got in here. Hmmmph. I t only took a few pulls for him to come. He would then skeet all over my face. Since the sink didn't work, I had to use the letter from my baby to clean it off.

_____ walks into our cell and starts an argument. I am obliging everything he asks because I'm not in the mood to play "wifey" tonight. He grumbled something, but I ignored him. As soon as lights out, he grabs me by the throat and sticks his tongue in my ear. Strength from some part of my hidden gender begins to brew. I faintly hear the drums in my mind. I imagine being on the Seranghetti with my spear in one hand and my shield in the other. Beads of many colors and shapes adorn my neck. My sheath is dangling on my right side. The dingy loin cloth that barely covers my manhood, sways with my movement. I thrust towards my prey. A great lion has posed a threat to my village and family. I must garner all my skill as a hunter to stop him. He lunges at me, but to no avail. The cold steel of my blade finds his abdomen. I snatch it out and plunge it into his back. He staggers to the ground and quivers in angst.

As I stand over him to assure his demise, I can see the life draining from his eyes. With his last instinct of fight he stretches out his mighty paw to strike me in the head. With all of the warrior in me I plunge the blade deep into his heart. I see that the hunter has subdued his prey. So as my cell is stormed by COs, I drop the shank. They drag me out and handcuff me. One of them sees the blood leaking from the wound on my head. He asks if it was mine or _____. I blank out when I come to I am lying in the infirmary.

# Loves Triangle

I love him more for what he is not.

He isn't smart.

He isnt't perfect.

He isn't faitful.

He isn't kind.

As a matter of fact, he isn't someone
you would even consider rialble.

I hoped he wouldn't succeeed, and then
he would always have a need for me.

I wish I was his "one".

I would always sit and imagine what it would
be like to be on the other side. The side that he
is cheating on. The side that he ignores me for.

The side that drins his continuously erect penis.

The side that makes him ipe my tears.

The side hat makes him make
Saturday morning breakfast.

The side that makes him click over on the phone.

The side that makes him answere my
texts.the dies te makes him smile.

The side that makes him call me his baby.

The died that holds me ht entire night.

The died that freaks me in the morning.

The side that makes him claim me
in the presence of the others.

The the side that he will go hungry for.

The side that he will lose sleep for.

The side hta he will die for.

Here iam alone again.

I told him tah I wanted to be left aolone.
He had insisted tah we could have a good
life together, but I was so wrapped up
in my own shit until I could not see it.

I looked past him, and at another.

He made me feel a way the other couldn't

I listened to all the voices in my imagination
and kicked him out of my life

I insisted he pay all the bills, and get my
hair done one more time, then made
him leave his key on the crecdenza.

He nodded his head and did not protest.

I heard a familiar song on the radio.
That was what he used to tell me. I let
him go. I chose theo ne in the bush
andtossed the one in my hand.

I'm so alone.

Tears flow without coercion.

I'm so alone.

The one I let go is now snug and comfortable
with a woman who appreciates him.

A woman who loves and respects him.

She even accepts his wisdom as truth.

He's happy and warm.

I am cold and alone.

I wanted someone who would be there.

Who would take care of me
when times got hard.

Someone who whould hold my hand who would
understand mw when the world didn't get me.

Someone who cared enough to try and make
it right when things between us went wrong.

I had him and let him go.

When he was with me, everyone called.

Girlfriends wanted to hang out.

Men shistled andwanted my number.

They just had to have them some me.

They needed what he possessed.

I was the cure to all their ills and they had to have me.

My phone rang incessantly.

I had to turn it off to get some peace.

Now I turn it on just to hear the ringtone.

Just as swiftly as the bird in the bush took flight, so did my popularity.

No one cares.

No one calls.

No one whistles.

No one needs me.

No one pays attention when I talk.

No one looks at me when I walk by.

I have once again become the one on the other side.

The one who gets hang up on.

The one who is pushed to the side when his main woman walks in.

The one who has to cry alone.

The one who has no hand to hold .

The one who has to wash her own car.

Take in her own laundry.

Who has to take care my own self when I am sick.

This saga will continue until I learn the difference between what is and what could be.

# I Tried

I just spent six years of my life in a loveless marriage. It ended when he came and told me that his girlfriend was tired of me getting all of his attention. He then packed what few things he had left at home and then bid me a final farewell.

That's when I heard him call.

It's not the first time. He had been after me for years. He started woo-ing me the year I turned seventeen. See, growing up, I was an only child. My mother was a junky who could barely get out of her own way. My father obliged her habit to ease the guilt of never being around for either of us. What few friends I could coax into playing with me were gone just as soon as they collected the toys shoes, or clothes I would purchase for them. Hmmph,…you know that joke about having to buy friends, that was me. Back then he would call me every day. I was just a child and all I needed was love. All I needed was just one person in this life who would love me. He promised that he would be gentle, and that I could rest in his arms. I had danced with him a couple of times even held his hand but I never dreamed of leaving with him.

As I sit here quietly sipping my tea, he whispers my name again. I want to answer, but....i-l-m not sure if I am ready to go. He reminds me that he is the only person who loves me. My Andy is gone. The one I had given my love and life to unconditionally just told me I wasn't good enough. All the pain I had tucked away since child hood. All the anguish I had stored from my teen years, and even the sorrow I hid from my beloved Andy's departure washed over me. I stand up as if to say come and take me! I'm yours!

He entered the room. He immediately removed his top hat. He's such a gentle man. He was tall, pale, and thin but his shadow was heavy and it covered the room with a dark and sterile calm. He stretched out his gnarly fingers as it to say come to me baby girl. I felt free. I felt wanted. I felt an urge to sleep. Perhaps I was finally home with him. Maybe this is where I belonged. It could have been the poison that sweetened my tea. All I know is I was finally home in the arms of Death. I tried to elude him for years. I ran I hid. I ignored his constant pleas, but no more. My only suitor has claimed his new bride.

# Later that day...

I knew I should have waited to tell her. It was inevitable. We were growing apart. When we first started dating, her wholesome behavior was endearing. Now I feel like I am trapped in the sixties. She is so attentive that she smothers. I know she wants the best for me, but I don't need another mother. There is no girlfriend. Maybe I should have just been honest. I knew it. When I told her that I was leaving, her face just dropped. I didn't know how low until I heard her crying in the kitchen. My poor baby... I still love her she just doesn't fit into my life anymore. God let her be ok!

Just then he doctor comes in."Mr. Ramses?"
"Yes doc how is she?"
"Well we were able to stabilize her, and she should be coming around in couple of hours. When she wakes up we will put her in a room. Getting the poison out her system was easy, now getting it out of her mind is another issue. Suicide attempts are nothing more than a cry for help. Had you noticed any unusual behavior? Has she been depressed or withdrawn lately?"
"Yeah." I didn't want to tell this stranger all of our business.
"Well, as I said, she should be coming around again."
I reached for his hand and thanked him. I was so relieved that my baby was going to be ok. What am I going to do right now? I have made

arrangements to start my new life. How am I going to do this?

"Andy?"

I was so engrossed in thought I didn't see her standing there.

"Hey lady!"

"I was on my way to see a client, when I saw you speaking with the doctor. Is everything alright

I wasn't sure how to answer that question. I knew Jessica from school and she always seems to have it together. With all that's happened I don't know if I can trust her. She sensed my hesitation.

"Do you need some privacy?" She interrupted my thoughts. I answered with a bit apprehension.

"Not to be rude, but yes."

"Say no more. I am a grief counselor, and I am doing some consulting for the hospital. Listen, I have to run, but if you feel the need to reach out, here's my card." She turned to walk away before I could respond.

Just then the ICU nurse walks over to me and tells me that my wife has been calling out for me. I jump to my feet and practically run to her bedside. What was I thinking? How could I do this to her? Will she ever forgive me? However long it takes I will make this up to her. I look down at my baby's face an see how weak she seems. Her lips looked parched and usually glowing skin looked grayish and sallow. She opens her eyes and looked straight at me. At least I thought she was looking at me. I call her name. She doesn't respond.

"Is someone there?" She asked weakly.

I wave my hands before her face. No reaction. I push the button to call the nurse. I finger the card with Jessica's information on it. I wonder if she is still in the hospital.

## Switching things up...

I saw his hand wave before my face, I just chose to ignore him. I'll show him. If he thinks he's going to just up and leave me, he's got another thing coming. I have given up too much to just let some other tramp have him. I love him with all my heart and I don't want to live without him... and I won't let him live without me. "Baby, it's me. Andy. Can you see me?

He places his hand on my shoulder. I flinch.

"Is someone there?" I asked in the most pitiful voice tone I could muster. I managed to make my body tremble, and I start to ease away from his touch. "Please, don't hurt me. I'm waiting for my husband please. I begin to sob.

He walks away from my bed side to a distant corner of the room. I try to listen to his conversation. From what I could tell, he called someone named

Jessica. That must be the tramp he's leaving me for. Not today honey he has to stay and take care of his sick wife.

He walked back to my bed side and places that hand on my shoulder again. I shudder form his touch not because I am pretending, but because he just has that effect on me.

"Sweetie I don't know if you can hear me, but we are going to get thru this together." He began to cry. I wanted to comfort him so much, but at the same time, he deserves to suffer after all he has put me thru.

As he is holding me in his arms, I hear a knock on the door. I have to catch myself from yelling come in, so I fake a cough. The door opens and in walks one of the most beautiful women I have ever seen. She had the cutest little hour glass figure, chocolate brown skin and a meticulously cut hairstyle. Andy jumped up and immediately ran to greet her. I was so jealous that there was probably smoke coming out of my ears. What the hell does he think he is doing calling his whore to my bed side. I'll fix him.

# A change in the game plan...

It's been two weeks since they released me the from the hospital. My plan to trick Andy into staying with me was foiled when the doctor came in and caught me off guard a couple of times. At first it was easy. All I had to do was just play it cool and stay in character. Lying is not an easy chore, and it is my first time playing the bad girl role.

Now I am on to bigger and better schemes. Every morning at six I go in the bathroom and throw up. He hasn't touched me in 2 months, but I am determined to keep my man. If he doesn't ask me what's wrong soon I am going to throw myself down the back stairs. There are only 6 steps and the only chore would be landing. I have got to fall just right to make sure I break a leg or at least my hand.

"G'morning hon!" I smile as I greet him.

"Hi." He answered dryly. I continue, "I haven't been feeling well lately. Baby I think…I think I may have a stomach virus or something." I place my hand on my stomach to direct his mind to that train of thought.

Andy goes to the refrigerator, grabs the orange juice and takes a healthy swig, throws it back on the shelf, and then slams the door shut. He then looks at me with the most peculiar glance, belches, and walks out of the kitchen. There he plops down on the sofa, and grabs the remote. He has been nesting on the sofa since he brought me back to our home. Before the accident, he always had some where to be, or something to do. Now all he does is sulk. If I can just get him excited about this baby then…what am I saying? I am starting to believe my own hype. Maybe I should let him go. I want him to be happy. He barely talks to me when he is here and when does he only asks me what's for dinner or where is the clean laundry. I only want what's best for him. I thought if he saw me in a different light, he would stay. I need him to need me. What am I thinking? Of course he should be free! Then when he sees how good I take care of him he'll come crawling back to me.

Just then, I hear his cell phone ring. I ease over to the door of the living room and listen.

"Hey lady!" he exclaims.

That's the first time he's smiled since I have been home.

# Not another lecture...

"Hey girl! I was just about to call you and see what time we are supposed to be meeting for lunch."

It always took me forever to get dressed. After all, I have an image to uphold, there is not a day that goes by that I don't thank GOD for blessing me with such good looks. I'm not trying to brag I just know what I've got.

"Well you know me. Listen I have a meeting right after so it will have to be a quick lunch." I knew Pat was in one of her "reading" moods. She was all too willing to read me the riot act about my involvement with Andrew.

I was meeting my "next". He is trapped in a

loveless marriage with a pilgrim, whose idea of fun is quiltin' and barn raisin'. He is waiting for the perfect time to let her down easy. The last time he tried to leave, she tried to kill her fool self. I hate to seem selfish, but if she hadn't done that, then I would not have connected to that fine Andrew. He and I have a few classes together. I am feeling a whole lot closer to him since she got out of the hospital. Every day he calls me and we pray together. I counsel him about his relationship issues and as a result I know exactly what he is looking for in a mate. It's just a matter of time before I scoop him up.

## Lunch at LuLu's

"Hey Pat!" I greeted my best friend.

Patricia Jameson was my oldest and dearest friend. One day in the 3rd grade, Bobby Wilkins made me eat a caterpillar in front of our PE class and she rescued me. She rushed right over grabbed his ear and yanked it until he cried uncle. After she finished kicking his butt, she made him apologize to me and made him promise to be my boyfriend. That was all good until he peed in his pants at our annual snake show. He then became a nerd and I broke up with him. That lasted until our junior year in high school. His parents hit the lotto, and he once again became the BMOC.

Pat was the only one who could reach me spiritually. She grew up in a very religious household. Her mother and father both co-pastored a holiness church. I became saved as a result of hanging around Patricia. My relationship with GOD has grown, but sometimes I just need a break from all his religious stuff. I have some habits that make it hard for me to qualify for a halo, but I do alright.

"Baby girl I don't mean to pry, but you have got to give up this Andy guy."

Pat always felt the need to mother me. Contrary to what she might think, she is not my mother! She needs to mind her own damn business!

"Pat I love you girl, but I have this situation under control." I grabbed a menu and pretended to be perusing the cuisine. "Oh they have those crab cakes you like so much."

"Forget the crab cakes! This man is in a relationship with a very sick woman. A woman who I might add has tried to take her own life. Sweetie, if she has no regard for her own life, what makes you think she would care anything for yours?"

I can't stand this. "Pat let's not go down this road again. I got this thing with Andrew under control."

I signaled for the waiter.

"I will have the cob salad, no beans...umm, sweet tea and for dessert..."

Pat interrupted. "Sir, could you give us a moment?"

I cut her off before she could start up again. "Patricia listen, I am not going to debate this with you! My mind is made up. I am not going to stop seeing Andrew because he needs me right now. So just change the subject. Besides I am starving!" I signaled for the waiter once again. Simultaneously, Pat held up her hand to stop him from approaching.

"Mark my words you will regret continuing to see this man. He is not much of a man if he cannot share his feelings with this woman. If he is that weak with his current relationship, why in GOD'S name would he all of a sudden grow a spine with you?"

I am so tired of talking about this with her. As she continues to cut Andrew up, I continue looking thru the menu with intensity. I was not going to justify my love for Andy to someone who could never understand it.

As the waiter takes our orders I fall silent. She knew that this was a sure sign of anger with her for butting in my personal affairs. I suppose that is what a true friend would do. She knows me better than most and has been there for me during some pretty rough times. But I am my own woman. I say how I will live my life. Our food arrives and we begin to eat in silence. The air between us is thick as fog. I can be downright stubborn at times. I would have gone the entire meal without so much as a grunt.

"Well I see you have made up your mind. That's the last you will hear about his from me. She summoned the waiter back to our table. When she waved her hand, I felt a sliver of ice shoot through my soul. I instinctively look around the restaurant. I didn't see anything, but for some reason I felt a dark cloud lurking in the air.

# The lunch date

I have no other words to describe how I am feeling all the time. This the kind of tired that sleep won't cure. Sometimes I wish that she had been successful at killing herself. At least then she would be out of pain.

It's not that I don't love her I just can't turn pity into a relationship. She can't see that she is pushing me away with all of these lies she keeps telling. I know good and damn well she's not pregnant. I hadn't touched her in almost two months. That's why didn't respond to that madness in the kitchen. Next thing you know she'll be looking for some other symptoms to add to all the fake vomiting she's been doing in the morning.

The message light goes off on my cell phone. It's Gerald. This tall chocolate brother in my psychology class was sending me a text. He has been real instrumental in helping me get thru this drama. Talking with him is the only bright spot in my day.

To keep her from thinking we are going to be a couple again, I answered Gerald with "hey lady". This keeps her mind on the other woman. She has no idea about me. Before my wife got sick, we had planned to take a trip to Atlanta. He has a frat brother there who plays for the Hawks and we were going to make a weekend of it.

'meet me at LuLu's'

I wonder what he's got going on.


## How it all goes down...

Why didn't I just let him go?

I saw them walking out of LuLu's and I completely lost it. I should have just let him go

"You have the right to remain silent..."

He said they just bumped into each other, and that he was walking her to her car.

"You have the right to an attorney..."

I saw the body laying there in a puddle of blood. Hmmph...just think I put that box cutter in my purse by accident. I was bringing it back home to help Andy unpack.

"Ma'am step this way. Watch your head."


## Earlier that evening...

"Hey man!" this is a whole new lifestyle for me. I get a rush every time I am near him. If he wasn't in my life I don't know what I would do.

"So are you ready to hit the road?"

Where are we going?"

A-town boy!" he exclaimed and pointed to the whimsical "A" on his hat.

I thought about the last time I tried to leave home. A pain of guilt shot through my chest.

"Naw." I could have retold the story of how my unstable wifey almost offed herself when I decided to leave, but it was a sad and sordid song that I was tired of singing.

"Man you have got to let this shit go!" He took a sip of his beer and sat back in the booth. He didn't look at me just then, but I could see him clenching his jaw. God I love this man!

"Baby.." I stopped immediately. He shot me this look of surprise and fear as he looked around the restaurant. We are a couple yes, but not in this small town. That is why he is so anxious for us to get to Atlanta. There we will be surrounded by men who think like us. Here, in this God forsaken town, men love other men, but they keep it on the hush.

"I am ready to go. I just don't know how to leave. You know last time she..." again I stopped.

"Well I am growing tired of this whole scene. Either you coming with me or you gonna stay here in misery?" He paused and looked me square in the eyes, " I got to go to the john." He slid out of the booth and walked away. I LOVED to watch him walk away. He's right. I got to figure out a way to get out of this place. Not just this town, but this place of secrets, lies, duplicity and duality. I cannot hold this relationship with Lynn together anymore. I have to let her go. Right then and there I vowed to tell her when I got home. Not just that I am leaving, but why. I can't wait for my man to come back so I can tell him to start packing.

## Meanwhile at another table...

Pat sat in silence. I hated it when she gave me the silent treatment. Her silence was almost as bad as her yammering about Andy.

"How are the crab cakes?" I asked trying to ease the mood

"Their alright." She was determined to make this difficult.

"Alright...I hear you." I hated to admit this to her, but she was right.

"Say again?" Now she was just being sadistic.

"I said I hear you. I will stop seeing Andy. I know he is no good for me and I will stop interaction with him immediately." I begin to sulk as if I were an unruly child who just got spanked.

"Well, I know this was a hard decision to make, but I'm glad you came to your senses." She wiped her mouth and took a long swig of iced tea. She picked up the soup spoon and took two healthy slurps of tomato bisque. I love my friend, but she eats like a little pig.

"I know you are looking for 'Mr. Right', but you are not going to find him. He has to find you. The bible says "HE" that findeth a good wife findeth a good thing. Stop looking and wait."

"Well Pat that's easy for you to say, you already have someone special. I go home alone every night and frank I am really tired of waiting. Happiness isn't going to just stroll right up to me. I have got to go out there and grab it." She was always trying to tell me how to live. I know one thing; this is the last lunch she and I will ever have.

Pat was up on her high horse and she continued to lecture me on an already closed subject. "We are not talking about a job or a degree where you are supposed to apply such tenacity. We are talking about the love of another human being. Even in the bible, we see where Eve was given to Adam. God didn't place her in the garden and told her to go seeking! Instead he formed her from a rib and set her in his path. You have got to maintain your strength and wait for your Adam to find you."

As much as I hate to admit it, Pat made perfect sense.

## On the other side of town...

"I don't feel like cooking. There is not enough of anything in this house to make dinner anyway." I said to myself while probing the fridge. I walk over to the drawer where we keep all the takeout menus. We haven't had take out in a while. I look up at the clock. I have just enough time to run out and grab something before Andy gets home. Hmm.... pizza, tacos, burgers, aha!...LuLu's. It's Andy's favorite restaurant.

Look at all of these boxes. Andy said he was going to unpack when he got the chance to pick up a box cutter so he can break them all down. I will stop and pick one up. Wal-shop is a block away from LuLu's. I will put in the call so the food will be ready when I get there. This is our night. I feel so liberated and frisky. I am starting to believe things will be changing for us soon.

## The beginning of the end...

As pat grabs the check from the table, I look across the restaurant and I see Andrews. He is dining with a very handsome, athletic, chocolate man. Just as soon as I spot him, he spots me. He waves. Pat returns and drops a five on the table. She sees me glancing at Andrew, and starts in again, but this time I stop her. For the first time I see what he really is. I should have known, but then I have never seen him interact with other males. Oh well this is the perfect time to tell him that I want to discontinue our friendship. What would it matter to him anyway? Wow I feel sorry for his wife now. She has no idea.

He saunters over to me and gives me one of those Joan River's air hugs.

"Hey sweetie!" he kisses me on the cheek. 'SWEETIE'? Now that's the first time he's ever said that, but then again I haven't seen in his element. Just as he places his hands around my waist, in walks his psycho wife.

I knew it!!! That skank is after my husband! I shove my hand in my purse and take that box cutter out of its wrapper. I instinctively turn and walk back out the door. I will wait until walks out and meet her at her car. I will show her. That's MY husband!!!

# My Cubby Hole

How do you get through the nights? I know that
joy is emmminent. There is always light at the end
of that tunnel, but what do you do for the duration
of the ride. I think it's the waiting that eats at your
core. That rise of nervous energy that pushes you
to eat, smoke, shoot up, or reach for hat pipe. You
got to wonder about the mean time in between
time. Damn right its mean time. I imagine that I
am a seed that gets buried in that cold wet dirt.
Harassed by earth worms and scorched by the
sun it pushes an strains until it gets through to the
surface, but wait,...it's not quite spring yet, and
when it gets through a rough patch of dirt it's
cold and lonely because no others are peeking
through. It should die; its supposed to die, but
because it has strong roots it endures the icicles
forming on its tender green leaves and those harsh
winter winds. Only to become dormant not dead

which death would be more merciful, but it has to see. It is fully aware of its purpose to reproduce, so it holds on and continues to strain. Then the rays of the spring sun start to warm it, only to be followed by rain, rain, and more rain. Right before it drowns, the sun moves closer and dries the earth's tears and before he knows it, it's hot!

The sun is scorching once again its tender parts. Even as the seedling begins to rise and spread its flowers majestically there are now predators. Winged, stinging beasts that land without warning and tear into its bark leaving holes. These shallow dents in its character are boring seething scars that never quite heal. The little sapling recovers somehow and reaches upward or so he thinks , poor thing is heavy with growth and does not know that he's leaning to one side. Life continues, but at an odd degree. Someone eventually has pity on the budding sapling and places a stick there but forgets to tie the two together. Using his compadre as a guide he pushes once again upward.

And there I am. My life in a nutshell. Pushing upward; always reaching always growing heavy with purpose. I'm going to start my story not quite at the beginning. I mean let's face it, most don't remember their true beginnings so I'm going to start at the point where I was pestered by my first earthworm:

It was circle time and this little ashy by named

Teddy had just pooped in his pants to the tune of "Games people Play". I was afraid of him from then on. Every time he came into the closet where we hang our jackets or in to the cafeteria, I would get nervous. I didn't know that God was trying to tell me something about life, because from that day to this shit has just happened. Later that day, two of the older girls came up to me and started pushing me around. One of them took my juice at snack time and the other one wiped a bugger on me while we were finger painting. Relina Watts and Angie Hairstein were their names. These two bullies made life for me fairly difficult and began the trend of picking on the young, helpless one. Relina was a thin, dark complexioned, nappy headed imp who had a speech impediment. Her little cohort, Angie was a peach colored girl who was as plump as a little ginny. And she was just as gullible. She had long hair and was the most attractive of the two. They came back to the cubbies where I was trying to color a picture of a dancing clock. Relina said toAngie, " Eggie do it do it, her can't tell!"

When Relina opened her hand she had a piece of gum that she had been chewing. Angie took her gum out of her mouth and stuck together with Relina's gum. They then took both wads and stuck it in their panties. She rolled it around in her little pissy twat then she handed it to Angie who did the same. After it was saturated with five year old snatch they stuck it in my mouth, and made me chew it. I was only 3 at the time and I knew nothing of right or wrong. I was weak and ripe to be badgered.

Just as I was turning the corner, I saw her. It had been years since I had laid eyes on that witch. I could still see those ashy lips and pic-a-niny hair thru the camouflage of make-up and tacky clothes. I was at the check-out counter TJ Maxx. She walked aimlessly towards me with her cart in tow. She stared directly at me, her eyes boring another hole in my soul. The right side of her lip began to curl in a half smile. She knew who I was. That bitch! Yeah, I see you too. She walked right past me almost in slow motion. My soul was yelling at my body to run and walk the other way. I could not. I had made myself a vow. I had planned it so many times, especially when yet another thing went wrong in my topsy-turvy life. I had to do this to set things back in balance. She deserved it. After all, she wasn't the only one. Fate had taken care of Angie. Her husband had contracted HIV, and passed it on to her. She died 2 years ago. But that black moppet Relina was still skirting thru life, no doubt tormenting others with her disdain and smugness.

I forgot about my purchases, and followed her.

"Ma'am! Ma'am your bags!" The cashier frantically called after me. I took the packages and walked out the door. I was so enthralled in my thoughts, that I sat them on the nearest bench. I did not want to lose Relina. I followed her thru the parking lot. She parked in a handicap space. I took note of her license plate number. DP136L. I took note of the make and model: Chevy Tahoe. I was parked a few rows over so I made a mad dash for my own vehicle. I watched that tramp open the gate and put packages in the rear. She didn't' have a care in the world. She had no idea this was her day to pay. Death was swooping in on her like an eagle on a snake.

She went quickly. I slit her throat and watched her bleed out. Every drop of blood was a representative of all the others who died because of her foolishness. Before I took her life, I shoved my fingers in her snatch and made her taste it. The same thing she did to me years ago. That tramp liked it. She thought this was the norm. That heifer even tried to use reverse psychology on me, but my mind was already gone. So she didn't have a whole lot to work with. After I shred her juglar, I felt a long waited release. All the victims were cleansed from my knife. I didn't have to imagine her face. I saw the life drain from her face, with it came my peace. I was then ready to go too.

I take out my cell phone and call my lady.

"Hey honey, how's my girl? Listen baby, I just had some last minute details to attend to, but I will be home and in your arms within the hour. I love you sugar." I always felt a pang of guilt after...you know. She was the only thing keeping me form going on a murderous rampage and destroying the very city where I grew up. Teddy told me years ago to leave and start over somewhere else.

I started thinking about the love of my life. Ironically I met her because of the death of another. He was her husband. She didn't know I was the one who pulled the trigger or she probably would have cleansed her soul as well. There was something so pure about death. It was a chance to start all over again in another dimension. Perhaps in the next lifetime Relina will think twice about taking advantage of the weaker ones.

# Teddy Bare

Now would be a good time to introduce myself. My name is Theodore Rawlinson, and I am a product of Nurture vs Nature. Meaning if my whore of a mother would have nurtured me as a baby, I wouln't have this out of control nature. Church is a terrible place where terrible people go to hide their indiscretions. I know because I am currently sucking the pastor's dick. He gets in the pulpit and makes these big pouring speeches about God making Adam and Eve, not Adam and Steve. Then once he exits and goes to his study, I get on my knees and try to change his mind.

No one really suspects me because I am one of his nurses. He has the church and first lady believing that he has to come down off his glory before he can fellowship. So like a fool she leaves me alone in his study so I can help him release his "glory". One time he told his wife he had to spend the night with me to keep the demons from beating me physically. What he didn't tell her was that he put those bruises on me and wanted to spend the night so he could try out all I had to offer him. He told me that "head" wasn't getting it anymore.

She is so dumb. Most women are. They can't see the forest for all those damn tree limbs blocking their view. Like when her man is always hanging around a gay man, talking on the phone to them, even when he is talking on the phone to his lady and she criticizes another gay man, if he takes offense to it, you guessed it,...HE'S GAY!!! No he's not being a good "friend", nor is he just looking out for a homey. He's around this particular set of sissies because he is bi-curious, or he is outright gay.

Most men get caught up in this lifestyle because they don't have strong father figures in their lives. It's kind of like learning to pee standing up. Some domineering man-lover will take the weaker under his wing and somehow make him feel validated. This man will provide a world of acceptance and ease for a confused, hurting weak man. Then he will introduce him to this next level sex. I enjoy me some pussy, but making love to a man is some next level shit. Why did God make this feel so good if it was so wrong? I know the bible says that it is an abomination to God for man to lay with another, but I am just gone. I could go on and on about this, but there is so much more for me to tell. I even had one of my dear girl friends ask if I thought her man was gay because he made a joke about sucking another man's dick....HEL-LLLOOO!!... Wake up Pollyanna! That sister is waiting for the whole tree to hit her before she gets the point.

Ladies, there is no such thing as a used to be gay man. He either is or he isn't. If he is honest enough to say he has been with a man, then don't think there is nothing you can do to stop him from loving any other man. He may choose To stay hetero, but after a while the craving of another hard body against his own will over power whatever love he may feel for you. Only another man can love a man the way a man supposed to be loved. Don' let these queen ass niggas tell you that it's about feelings and all that other bullshit. It's about the dick, the whole dick, and nothing but a dick! There are some men who are effeminate, but are not gay. They are just a messy, talkative, or even as dramatic as females, but are not a part of the community. Then there are those who are a part of the community, but don't know it yet.

Oh yeah, I'm supposed to be telling you how I came to know that last bitch. Well I am the kid who shitted in his pants at circle time. Who knew I would impact someone so deeply. She was afraid of me for a while, but she started to come around.

My contempt for the church and women

began when I was 4. We were all at vacation bible school and some of the older kids started to tease me. I was a little chunky boy that had a rash across my forehead from ringworm and I smelled like pee. My momma was so nasty even the roaches in our trailer had on house shoes. I always had on high water pants, ashy hands and feet with no socks.

This 14 year old named Boochie would pick on me every chance he got. While we were on a break, he walked over to me, knocked my squeeze cup out of my hand, and commenced to shoving me around. Even though this was church, these little demon children loved to see someone get hurt or beat up. Boochie was not satisfied until he had thrown me to the ground.

"Get up Pee-bird!" he yelled. This was the nick name he gave me.

"Get up before I kick your ass!" How easy is it to intimidate a 4 year old? You got to be pretty lame to make a baby your target. It turns out he was just being a boy...you know stupid. He liked me and didn't like the fact that he liked me, so I became the brunt of all his disdain.

"Aaah-haha! Look at Pee-bird" Aletha Barnes would laugh at anything. She was just as homely as I was, but she stayed under the radar by keeping everyone laughing at me.

When it was time to go back into class, Ms Rita rang the chimes and called out to us. Boochie had other plans for me. He grabbed my head covering my mouth and shoved me into a closet. That's where he made me get on my knees and give him head. This wasn't the first time. He got me once during a choir rehearsal. The only difference this time was we had an audience. I heard them giggling on the other side of the door.

"Let me see" that was the voice of Aletha. I heard her giggle once more. The next voice I heard was that of Jimmy. He was Boochie's cousin. He snatched open the door and yelled, "Ima tell!" I was terrified. While the door was still open, Lenny, Jimmy's best friend rushes in and slams the door behind him.

"I told you he had a deep throat." Boochie bragged. From that moment on they took turns in my mouth. Nobody came to rescue me from these thugs. I was at their whimsy. I vowed then and there to help the little guy. Nobody would ever feel like this if I could help it. To top it all off, those kids told everyone what happened in that closet. I was even more of a cast off than before.

As was the rule my mother blamed me for making her look bad and beat blisters on me. Nobody made a fuss about such things in our home town. In most cases it was the norm. Hell I have even had relatives who have had children by their fathers and brothers. They were whispered about for a few weeks and then people just let it sink down into their memories. They don't really remember the details just that you were involved in something sleazy. I remembered. Every night

I wondered what it was about me that made people automatically mistreat me. Was I really that peedy or fat or dirty? I tried to be a friend to the ones who made a sport of tormenting me. I even obliged their sick deeds just to feel like I belonged. What did I know right... I mean nobody is all that good. That's why I got into the business

We were ostracized together, that's why we became so close. She and I decided to right all the wrongs that this world kept handing out to its victims. "Let's kill." She said without even blinking. We were in the 8th grade at the time. His name was Tim. He stole from peoples lockers and used to bully the smaller kids. We buried him behind the cafeteria wall. We then spread the rumor that he was talking about running away.

I started to explore more with boys then. It had gone beyond just giving head and into anal penetration. I was both, top and bottom. Boy pussy was just fantastic! I had some boyfriends my own age and some men too.

One of them was Cheryl's uncle. He would indulge us to pacify his guilt by buying us alcohol and marijuana. At first I thought he was interested in my mother, but he finally broke down and told me that he had a crush on me. I could full well understand, because I was the one who kept us above the water. I cooked, cleaned, and I worked at the grocery store part-time to keep us fed and to buy me some decent clothes for a change. I was no longer that little pee stained boy who took trauma from others, I was now a budding young man, who gave pleasure. Because of the filthy surroundings I was privy to, I had to have everything organized. My shoes were arranged by color and brand. My bed linens were so tight that you could bounce a quarter off my bed spread. Even my colognes were neatly spaced by the labels. If one of those things were out of place... whew! Let's just say it wouldn't be a pretty sight.

My mother had become a full blown alcoholic and continued to blame me for everything that was wrong in her life. When Wilson came along, she started to treat me nice again. He needed an excuse to be hanging around my house so I told him to act like he was interested in her. Whenever she passed out form all the liquor and coke he would feed her, he would head straight to my room.

As I mentioned before, I would work to keep us above the water, but it was my man who really held us down. Not because he cared anything about her, but because I treated him right. Needless to say she was my second victim. I finally grew tired of the beatings and scaldings with the hot water or burns with her cigarettes, so I put her out of her misery.

The dominate male figure that turned me out wasn't Wilson, it was Cheryl. She knew more about manhood than most. As a matter of fact the only things she didn't do was pee standing up. I lost my appetite for women when I turned four so our relationship was a different kind of love. Killing was how we expressed our love for each other. When I got caught selling drugs, she taught me to man up for prison. I could never have asked for a better friend...until she crosses the line.

# This Lil' Light of Mine

My story is not like all the others. See I was a good Christian girl. I went to church every Sunday and Wednesday. I was in at least three choirs, on the Jr. Usher board, and on the welcoming committee, I did the church announcements, and I was president of the YPD and whenever there was a program or a celebration I was the coordinator and the MC. In addition to working out my soul salvation, I was planning to be the first one in my family who was a virgin on her wedding night. I wanted to give my husband something nobody else had the privilege to know. I made God a vow that if he kept me from temptation, I would stay pure till the day I married. At least that was my plan until I met Stacks.

*This little light o mine,*

*Um gonna let it shine!*

This is how Sister Hawthorne started devotion as usual. I went to the bathroom and as I was shaking he excess water from my hands. Stacks darts across the curtain that divided the jr. and r. Sunday school classrooms and grabbed my booty. He squeezed it so hard that my knees buckled. I felt a stirring in my womanhood that ached for him to do more. He had been flirting with me off and on for the longest time. He only did it when no one else was looking though.

Stacks was green-eyed, dreamboat that was the object of every girl's fantasy in Ottawa County. He was a basketball player who could get any girl he wanted. I had seen him in the halls at school and often longed to be the girl on his arm. But alas, I was a skinny, knock-kneed little thing that had braces and a lazy eye. Stacks rubbed my humps so tenderly that my panties were soaked. I wanted to know about him in other ways. He was so cute with that sandy colored hair. Lord what I wouldn't give to kiss those soft supple pink lips of his. He grabbed my yet damp hands and took me out the side door. As we exited the back door, Deacon LG came around the corner and said, "Yall need to be back in church now."

"Yessah, we going." I chirped. I didn't know that stacks had other plans. As soon as we walked out the door, Stacks pushed me around the back of the building and up against the wall. He then looked me square in the eyes; just as a snake would charm his prey, and I couldn't move. As his beautiful eyes bored a hole through my soul, his hand wandered up my skirt. He felt the dampness on my panties and smiled at me. He put his hand under my chin and pressed those perfect lips against mine. I let out a small moan, and kissed him back with all the pleasure he bestowed on me. I forgot that I was behind the church, and that just on the other side of that wall service was going on. I caved into all the carnal lust that was burning inside me. I let down my guard and re-negged on the vow I made to God. I was playing into the hands of my secret crush and it felt so good.

Stacks massaged the lips of my vagina until neither of us could take it anymore. He then plunged his finger in my most valuable asset, (without my purity I was just another ugly girl). I moaned and leaned my head against his chest, surrendering my all to him. He then took his hand and led it to his crotch. I did not know what he wanted me to do with it so I just kind of grabbed at his bulging manhood. He was so hard, I lost my breath when he covered my hand with his and showed me how to stroke him. We fondled each other for what seemed like an eternity. He started to kiss me more passionately, and the pulses running thru me were getting harder and stronger. I thought I heard a door close, so I stopped and looked in both directions. This both angered and stirred Stacks to get more aggressive with me. He had caught a live one, and he wasn't about to let her get away. He thought like so many boys his age. Why waste your time with a ten when you can get two fives.

He started to ease my panties down. I hesitated at first, but we had gone past the point of no return. He eased them down past my knees and I wiggled out of one leg of them. He then unzipped his pants and let them fall open. He peeled his underwear back and his manhood pushed upward like a banana. The head of it was so perfect, I could not resist. I covered it with my mouth and tasted the sweet nectar that was emerging from the tip. He moaned and whispered a weak yes. I knew instinctively that I had him right where I wanted him. I could have asked him for anything then and his response would have been yes, a thousand times yes.

After I tasted his goodness, he picked me up spread eagle, and let his penis find its way to my portal. I cried with little yelps, which apparently touched his tender heart, because he held me closer as he introduced me to womanhood. He was very gentle as he poked and pushed past my hymen. He did this until he finally claimed my virtue. It was not as painful as I expected it to be. He slid in and out of me with ease, and every time he pulled out and pushed in he went deeper and deeper. I loved every stroke, and with every plunge, I felt closer to him. I released my inhibitions and started to push back against him. I rewarded his gentleness by grinding my hips into his. This seemed to weaken him more. Once again, I knew I had impacted him just as much as he had touched me. We climbed the ladder of ecstasy together rung by rung for what seemed like an eternity. Before we could reach heaven, we were interrupted by Deacon LG's gravelly voice.

We scrambled aimlessly to pull up our clothes and get back inside the church. He ran to the corner of the building and went back in thru the other side door. Before I could touch the door knob, Deacon LG grabbed my arm.

"Gal! Ima tell yo' mammy you 'round heh' screwing these lil' nappy headed boys!" He had a greasy face with a scar over his right eye. He had a dull bald head that came up to a point.

"I oughta whup you my'sef'" He gave me the most sinister look I had ever received from a man. He then looked me up and down and licked his lips. "Since you like fucking so much, Ima show you!" He snatched me by the arm and jerked me around, almost dragging me to the storage house behind the church. Once we got inside he started to yell at me again.

"I was watchin' yo' nasty ass the whole time. You let him stick it in you didn'ya!" I tried to rebut pleadingly, "Nosah! No-sah I didn't!"

"Yes you did you nasty ho!" Ho? Me? Was he taking about me? By the glower in his eyes, I knew my fate was sealed. In a rush I thought about the vow I had made to God and how carelessly I had broken it. I could remember none of the pleasure I was just feeling. My rendezvous with Stacks was a distant memory now. I was no longer on the flight to heaven, but on a rocket to hell. An eerie feeling ran up my back and I shook it off, and braced myself for what was about to take place.

He pawed at my breasts and handled me like a butcher. He literally threw my hands behind my back and snatched at my skirt. I stumbled across the nativity scene and he yelled, "Git up!" he shoved me past the cross we use during the Easter season and there in the presence of our Lord's shame he proceeded to give me my own. He unzipped his pants and shoved his piss stinking dick in my face.

During his assault, I was trying to remember that I was a good girl. He interrupted my thoughts "Open yo' mouf!" he yelled and slobbered at the same time. "Ima give you some real meat to chew!"

As I parted my lips this demon yelled at me once more "Suck it!"

The tears; somehow I remember the tears meeting under my chin. All I wanted to do was go back and right the wrong I had committed. I was always told it was a sin to make a vow and not fulfill it. It was better never to have made it in the first place. He shoved his stinky cock further down my throat, and damn near gagged me. He saw that I was trying to get away, so he grabbed the back of my head and shoved it in harder. "Good ain't it?!" That old goat asked as he scraped my chin with those warbled claws of his. I continued trying to free my elf. It wasn't' so much the head I was running from, but his nuts smelled like onions and I couldn't stand it any longer. As this musty nut gargoyle fucked my face, I tasted the most foul salty curds in this world. Here in his tainty sputum, was my punishment. As he came in my mouth, he yelled "Swallow it!"

As he fixed his clothes and I tried to gather what was left of myself respect, he bent over and snarled, "Now that will show you with yo' nasty self. You bet' not tell nobody. They won't b'lieve it no how. Ima upstanding man in dis' community. All I gotta do is tell 'em what I seen furst. Then they'd think you was just tryin' to get back at me."

He didn't have anything to worry about. I accepted this as my punishment. This is what happens when you break a vow to God. In my feeble brain, I reasoned that I deserved to have what began as a dream, to turn into a night mare. I pulled myself together enough to walk back in the service. Just as I was walking to my seat, I seen that old frog walk back to his seat. As he passed Stacks' seat, he patted him on the shoulder. I slid down on the pew because I felt like everyone knew what had transpired just now. How could something so sacred and beautiful turn to something so foul and disturbing? I felt like trash. Like all the plans God had for me were ruined and surely he wouldn't want to use a sinner like me. I asked him in my mind, would you please forgive me? His answer came in the most peculiar way. Mother Winston stood to testify and began quoting the scripture that there was now no condemnation to them who are in Christ Jesus.

# Moma's maybe Daddy's Baby

"Elma! Elma! Elmarrrrr!" Moma made it her daily routine to scream my name at lest twenty times.

"Check on them yonguns!" She dribbled out snuff spit and commenced to yelling again.

"Don't let my bread burn and sweep off dat back porch!" Do this. Do that . Hell I'd never even heard her normal talking voice. For the first fourteen years of my life I was nervous as hell. I eventually got use to it. By then I was shaking for a different reason because every time I left home and came back she was yelling and waiting for me to fuck up so she could whup me.

My momma thought that more she whupped me the better a mother she was. Judging from the scars on my back and across my face I would say she was past spectacular. But I knew in her own little strange way she loved me. She was only passing on to me undoubtedly what she got from her ma. When most people remember their memaws, they think of cakes and cookies baking in the kitchen, sweet words of wisdom, money in the handkerkchief, loving hugs and salvation from some serious ass whippings. Not in my stead. Mine was a gambling, shine, drinking shit starter who sic'd my momma on me every chance she got. She couldn't clean up or do noting that showed any mother wit. I hate to say it but I was glad when that old frog croaked. She was a royal pain in my already sore ass.

I was the oldest daughter of five siblings and I got stuck raising they bad asses. They never did anything I told them and whatever they did wrong, you guessed it I got the whipping. See my story is about being different. My mother, that poor white trash reject, got pregnant by a black man when she was thirteen years old. My dad found religion in Florida and left us alone after they threatened to lynch him. So my mother married the only red-neck in Tennesee who would have her. Of course he hated me, and to keep him happy she punished me repeatedly. When I turned thirteen, I got my period and a whole lot of trouble to boot. We are so country until we don't even have plumbing yet. One day I went out and peed on the back porch like I always do, when I dropped my dress tail and ran back to the stove to get supper started, I heard her always shrill voice.

"Gal! did you jus' piss out cher'?"

"Yessum." I answered with enough humility to keep her from jumping on me with a stick.

"Well go look in my chiferobe, and get one of them granny catcher. You done started. Don't piss out cher' no mo!"

I had no idea what she was talking about. Scared to death of asking I said, "Momma what's dat?"

"You done come to be a young missus so's you cant' pisss out cher' no mo'. You need to keep yo' bizness private."

"Yessum." I went to her chiferobe like she told me to. As I was digging thru the torn panties and lace worn slips, I found a little bag with those long white hospital pads. I opened one pad and pulled the tab off the back and stuck the pad to my little spread. I did not know that you were supposed to stick it to the seat of your panties. Shoot I only had three pair to begin with, and secondly I only got to wear them on special occasions. As I was walking back to the stove to start a fire, I saw Lemon, my step-daddy looking at me. He had an eerie presence about him that made chills run down my spine. No matter what I am doing, he always seemed to be somewhere close watching me. I hurriedly dropped my dress and grabbed up the wood. I scraped the bark off the dry pieces, and lit a match to it and while I was stoking the

115

fire Lemon came up behind and started sniffing my neck. As he rubbed his hand across my young flesh, I held my breath. The screen door creaked and momma walked in. he snatched his hand away from my back and pushed me away and reached for the poker.

"Git back gal! You don't know nothing about how to do nothing!" he growled.

Moma chimed in, "She is as useless as tits on a boar. Git in heh an' wah the m beans!" she always sided with him. That ensured his forgiveness and that he wouldn't find religion or anything else and leave her just as my daddy did. I been told I look a lot like him, perhaps that's why momma hates me so. Is it that she always catches Lemon looking at me. In any event I knew it would only take about two more of his comments about me before she grabbed a shoe, a belt or a broom handle and beat the hell out of me. I started to wash the peas. As I was putting them in the dish pan a great pain hit me in the stomach and I felt a gush between my legs. I kept pouring the water from the big white bucket all the while the blood was pouring down my legs.

"Gal look what you doin'!" water splashed on the floor as momma mauled and pushed my head. I dropped the bucket.

"Go put on sum step-ins you nasty coon!" As I was walking away the pad slipped and dropped to the floor. That was it. My ass whooping for the day. She grabbed a switch out of the corner (she kept some handy for just such an occasion) and proceeded to give me one of her special ass whippings. I called them special because when she whipped me in front of Lemon, she would hit me in the face, across the back, and in my head. She would even put her foot on my neck to show him my place in her life. Even though I was screaming my head off and trying to shield my face from the lashes, I could see him standing in the corner squinting his eyes and gritting his teeth at every lash, as though that would make it hurt me worse. I had news for both of them my pain went a lot deeper than those beatings and nasty comments. In my heart was a seed of bitterness that would make me repay them both for all the hell they put me thru.

This beating only lasted a few minutes. She must have been feeling merciful because I was menstruating. She beat me so bad one time, I had to stay home from school a month. I heard her tell Lemon that she was gonna beat the nigger out of me. It was just another tactic to break my spirit. I was too uppity. I had too much pride, she used to say. I needed to stay back so I could be the proper help when time came. Maidin' or working the fields all I would probably be able to do. She used to tell me that my color was an accident and that my place was with the rest of the riff-raff. Never mind that I had dreams of being an animal doctor or the person who designed them pretty buildings. When I told momma what I wanted to do she laughed and said, "That's too high a mark for a mulatto wench like you. You need to be looking for a nice colored man to settle down with and raise some younguns. Stay in your place gal she would say. Her hatred for me was so strong I could smell it some days.

Well after my beating, I gathered myself and headed for my room. As I was walking, I fell. The whole room was spinning. I tried to stand up again, but this time I threw up.

"What da hell is wrong wit' yun? Git yo stupid ass up an cleanup dis mess you done made." Lemon snarled at me. After I put on my step-ins, I took another pad out of momma's chiferobe. I figured out that the sticky part must go on the seat of the panties. All this was new to me. I had no idea what was happening to me. Yet I was afraid to ask because she always made me feel stupid.

Once I tried to write her a letter asking her about boys and what was going on with me. She scolded me and said she was going to make Lemon beat me when he got home. He was more merciless than she was.

Three years have passed since I started my cycle. I was trying to be a good girl doing everything momma wanted me to do and trying to keep those little bastards from tearing up what little we had. I also spent most days trying to keep Lemon off of me. Ever since that day at the stove, he has been hitting on me. Always bumping into or grabbing and pawing at my booty or worse trying to sneak a peek at me when I would take my bath on Saturdays. It seemed like he would pay more attention to getting plumbing or patching those holes in the roof and walls instead of just putting paste-board over them. When it rained we had more puddles inside than in the yard.

I wanted to tell momma about what he was doing, but there was the fear of another ass whipping. You know most girls my age were courting, going skating, to dances and having slumber parties, but I was stuck with those snot nosed brats. They had no respect for me because they were all white. They were Lemon's kids so naturally they were better than me. She told me on every occasion possible and always in their hearing she would refer to them as her children and talk down to me as if I was they slave mammy.

"It Sattiddy gal! Get them younguns ready for they bath. Yo taintey ass could stand a little water too!" Momma croaked.

I put on the big pot on the stove and got the white bucket and headed for the flowing pump. As I was filling they bucket, Lemon was chopping wood. He stopped, wiped his brow and then started studying me up and down. A chill ran down my back. There was a strange feeling I had. That bastard wasn't long off my ass. I actually woke up one night to him rubbing my titties while he was jerking his dick. I started to yell but he cupped my mouth and pressed my head to the pillow. With this wicked look on his face I was all too familiar with, he would make it look like I had done something disrespectful and she, like the idiot she was, would believe him. " Lem" he stared at me with cold eyes as if to say 'shut yo' black mouth'. He went into their room next thing I know those familiar squeaks resounded thru our hollow house.

The baby was first, then the rest of the children, then me. That was standard practice in our house on Saturday. By the time I got to take a bath, the water was cold and murky. As I stepped in the tub, I caught a chill, so my nipples were erect. Lemon just came right out and watched. "Don't forget to get yo' cootey. I could smell you coming." He then looked me up and down licking his lips.

I just kept washing and scrubbing my yellow skin until it was as red as clay mud. It wasn't so much the dirt and grime from the past week, but it was the shame and poor treatment that I was trying to wash off with the already slimy water.

As I dried off Lemon walked by me, "Gal did you wash yo' ass? I still smell you com'ere!" Before I could answer, he grabbed my arm and spun me around, then he jammed his oily finger in my privates and smelled it. It wanted to cry out but what could I do? I was going to get a beating for being naked in front of her beloved Lem. After he digs around in me for a little while, he licked then smelled his finger. He made me feel so cheap.

Later that night he came to tuck us in. Once

again, I had to deal with his dirty hands pawing at my little nubs. This time he rubbed his dick across them. He then eased back the covers and started fondling my little bush. Next thing I knew he had picked me up and jammed me on his dick just to break the skin. I lost all feeling in my legs I had never known such pain.

Over the next couple of weeks every time momma turned her back he was getting on me. He was so quick on the draw that it only took about three seconds then he was spent. She must've gotten wind of his attractions to me. I stopped hearing those midnight squeaks. Momma's cussing and slapping me around got even worse. One day I walked in from school and she knocked me clean in the dirt because she couldn't find her snuff box. It was in the cupboard where it always had been. I couldn't say anything so I just took the beating. I knew what it was about.

It was alright though. Whenever she went on a rampage, I would ride lemon. One day she grabbed a switch to beat me for leaving he milk out, I lay down without any protest. As she beat and cussed at me I imagined me stroking her husband. That was sweet revenge. My coochie whipped him just like she beat me. For every lick she gave me I would stroke him so till he would shake like an old Maytag washing machine. It has been almost a year since I started fucking Lemon. He moved out of their room and took to sleeping on the couch. He used the lame excuse that momma's snoring was keeping him up at night.

She brought it on herself. I wanted to do more than just be average. I had become the whore she called me on many occasions. I won't be that way with our daughter, no sir! She is growing stronger every day. Just this morning I felt her first kick.

He is planning on leaving her soon. He told me we were going to Paducah Kentucky. He has friend who runs a mill up there. We got to hurry up though because my belly' getting bigger and I'm starting to show.